"Twenty seco

Livingston lo   eyers,
Lambert, Ogan, and Colon."

"Ten!"

Weyers yelled through the cloth covering, "Don't hesitate!
Go out, turn facedown, count to ten, then pull the cord."

"Go!"

When he hit the ground, reality returned with a jolt. Livingston didn't see the parachute, but he heard and felt it. It
drew him to his feet, and he limped forward as he struggled
to pinch the quick-release hook. When the chute finally came
off, he scooped up the lines and hauled in the deflated canopy.

Lambert was chattering from the cold. Livingston handed
him his own gloves, then bundled up the parachute and
stuffed it behind a skimpy bale of hay. They started toward
the field; as they passed the house, a shotgun blast was heard.

"Ahdyeen meenootah pahzhahloostah!"

Livingston looked toward the house, at the silhouette of a
man standing in the doorway. He had no idea what the
Russian had said; all he knew was that before he could reach
his Luger, either Lambert or he would be dead. . . .

FORCE FIVE
Destination: Stalingrad

Jeff Rovin

LYNX BOOKS
New York

DESTINATION: STALINGRAD

ISBN: 1-55802-165-5

First Printing/April 1989

This is a work of fiction. Names, characters, places, and incidents are either the product of the author's imagination or are used fictitiously. Any resemblance to actual events, locales, or persons, living or dead, is entirely coincidental.

This book is published by Lynx Books, a division of Lynx Communications, Inc., 41 Madison Avenue, New York, New York, 10010. The name "Lynx" and the logo consisting of a stylized head of a lynx are trademarks of Lynx Communications, Inc.

Printed in the United States of America

0 9 8 7 6 5 4 3 2 1

FORCE FIVE
Destination: Stalingrad

Prologue

Lieutenant Clayton Livingston sat at the desk in his London hotel suite, completing his report as he waited for the government liaison officials to arrive.

He shook his head. Just back from Algiers, from their first mission, everyone newly released from the hospital, and they were being sent away again.

That's the price you pay for being good. Getting another chance to be shot at.

Not that he was complaining. Compared to the desk job he'd left behind in the States, even KP would be an improvement.

Livingston finished writing about the destruction of the German airfield that had made an Allied landing in Algiers possible. Then he read what he had written: about having to fight the Germans after landing on the beach, sniffing out a traitor in the Algerian resistance, and working with erroneous intelligence, stolen explosives, and an airfield far more heavily fortified than reconnaissance had suggested.

He doubted that the new mission, whatever it was, would be better planned. Force Five had been put together *because* of problems in the system. There had been cracks in security, and men had had to be brought in from outside the intelligence service. Independent men who could think on the run. Two Americans—himself and the scrappy marksman Colon. Ogan, the by-the-book Englishman. Lambert, the conniving Frenchman. Weyers, the crackerjack South African pilot with fists the size of anvils.

An international team, to satisfy all the Allies. Expendable men, to satisfy the units that had given them up. Angry men, who didn't like the Axis or any of the crap they stood for.

Better planned? Who needed a better plan than a burning need to right the wrongs over here.

Livingston signed the report, then sat back. The satisfaction of having pulled off the Algerian mission was profound, and he savored it—though his gratification was tempered by the knowledge that as sharp as they'd been, they'd barely escaped with their lives, and would be damned lucky to do so again.

But he told himself that very few soldiers got to affect the outcome of the war single-handedly, and as different as each member of Force Five was from the other, that challenge had bound and inspired them like no other Allied fighting unit. It would do so again.

All things considered, he was looking forward to the return of his men from their one night's leave, and the arrival of liaison officers Sweet and Escott with information on the new mission.

Chapter One

"What do you think, Rotter? Has the blighter got the guts to show up?"

The speaker, a burly, young baldheaded man, ground a fist into his palm. Though Corporal Arthur "Wings" Weyers of the South African Long Range Desert Group was dressed in nothing but loose-fitting khakis, he didn't appear to feel the stiff, late fall wind that knifed across the wharf. He seemed aware of nothing but The Admiral's Pub on the other side of the dock.

Beside him stood a short, slender Frenchman with lively eyes. Corporal Jean-Pierre Lambert—known to his intimates as Le Rodeur, the Prowler—was dressed more sensibly than his companion, wearing a sweater and corduroy pants. He ground a cigarette under his boot.

"It isn't a matter of guts, *mon ami*. It's a question of brains. If he's smart, he'll stay in the bar. If he's brave, he'll come out and take his lumps. Either way, we win."

Weyers continued to punch his open hand. "I hope he comes out. I'd rather win by beating his brains out."

Several paces away, the third member of the party, Private Ernesto Colon, squatted on the icy wooden planks facing the Thames. Like Lambert, the American was dressed warmly, in a brown leather jacket and jeans. Un-

like the wiry Lambert, however, his posture, even in
repose, was taut, dangerous. He wore a brooding expression and said nothing, only stared out across the water.

After several minutes, the door of the pub opened and
three men walked out. Lambert recognized just one of
them, the red-bearded man on the left. He was Geoffrey
Thorpe, captain of the submarine *Saphir*. Just over a
week before, Thorpe had carried the five members of the
Force Five espionage team to Algiers, where they had
destroyed a German aerodrome. There had been no love
lost between the passengers and the captain, and tonight,
when Thorpe had happened to walk into the pub where
three Force Five men were celebrating their safe return,
Lambert had wasted no time inviting him and any two
of his crew members to come outside and air their grievances. Thorpe had agreed, and while the Force Five men
went outside, the captain had gone searching the smoke-
filled room for men.

Lambert whistled when he looked from Thorpe to the
captain's two companions. They were even brawnier than
the huge-shouldered officer.

Weyers muttered, "I didn't know they let bulls on sub-
marines."

"They don't," Lambert sneered. "Neither of those
men was on the minelayer. Looks like the bastard went
and got himself dockhands."

Colon came over, his concentration intense. "Does
that bother you?"

"No . . . it makes me *mad*. You can't even trust your
Allies to fight square."

Weyers drilled his palm one last time. "Doesn't matter. Let's go and knock out some—"

"Don't." Colon grabbed his arm. "I want you to stay
here."

"What?"

"When they get closer, grab the guy on the right, toss him to me, then hit the lug in the middle."

"Where will you be?"

"Behind you. We'll make it three-on-one before they know what hit 'em."

"Et moi?" Lambert said. "I get to handle Captain Le Porc?"

Colon nodded, then ambled behind Weyers.

As the sailors neared, their eyes reflected the searchlights that scanned the skies on the other side of the river. The men looked unearthly, like machines, and reminded Lambert of a robot he'd once seen in a German science-fiction movie.

"I found some mates," Thorpe said, grinning when they were just a few meters away. "Moby and Punch. They load mines for me—"

"—an' chew up airy-fairies like you in our free time," chortled the man who Weyers was supposed to grab. Lambert noticed an M tattooed on his forearm. This one must be Moby.

"I'll warn any fairies I run into." The Frenchman smiled. "Now then, monsieur, do you happen to know what we do in *our* spare time?"

"Sell yer mothers to sailors?"

"Mais non, monsieur. You mistake us for Englishmen. No. We go searching for blubber-gut mariners like you, and then we *harpoon* them."

The huge man glowered at Lambert, his heavy brow shrinking his eyes to small, black spots. "Why, you snivelin', goddamn frog—"

Before the man could finish, Weyers bolted forward and locked iron-strong fingers around his wrist, then tugged him ahead. Caught off balance, the man stumbled forward, where Colon was waiting. Sliding one hand in the man's belt and grabbing his shirt with the other, the American used the big man's momentum to pull him across the slick wooden dock. Moby hit the river with a heavy splash before his companions even realized what had happened.

The instant Weyers lunged, Lambert drove the toe of his boot into Thorpe's groin. The captain doubled over, and an uppercut to the jaw put him on his back. Meanwhile, rolling to the left, Weyers plowed his shoulder into Punch, sending the seaman to the ground. A knee drop to the stomach made sure he stayed there.

It was over in less than ten seconds, after which the three Force Five men gathered around Thorpe. The big captain was curled, fetuslike, and was clutching his crotch.

"Y' cheatin' bastards!" he moaned.

Colon's expression grew dark and he straddled the captain. "You're wrong, sir." He flipped out a switch-blade and put it to the man's chin. He had Thorpe's complete attention. "A cheating bastard woulda *stuck* you. All *we* did was teach you peaheads some manners."

Folding the knife away, Colon walked to the edge of the dock, where Moby was grasping at the pilings. Colon helped him from the icy waters, while Lambert went over to Punch. The man was winded but didn't seem badly hurt.

The captain climbed painfully to his feet. He smacked aside the helping hand offered by Weyers. "Tomorrow night, y' rat-bastards. I want ta see ya here same time— fair fight."

Weyers shook his head. "Sorry, but tomorrow night we head for parts unknown."

"Then when you get *back*," Thorpe growled. "We're in for a week o' repairs, an' we'll be waitin'."

The South African shrugged. "Fine with me. But I suggest you wait until the sub is fully operational." His wide mouth twisted into a vast, ungainly grin. "The only way you're going to knock down a Force Five man is with a torpedo. And you'd be smart to make it a direct hit, at that."

When Moby had been dragged onto the pier, and
Punch roused with a flurry of slaps, the victors headed
for the side street where they'd parked their black sedan.

"I liked that," Weyers said, pausing at the car and
looking back. "Damn, Rotter, but you know how to
show a body a good time."

They were unaware of a man who was standing in the
shadow of an old shuttered burlesque house, watching
their every move.

Wearing a tweed jacket and puffing hard on his pipe,
Inspector Bertram Escott of Scotland Yard marched stiffly
before his associates. His hands were locked behind his
back, and thick folds of flesh wagged to and fro beneath
his outstretched chin. Puffs of smoke rolled past his thin-
ning white hair and collected in a tester near the low roof
of the hotel suite.

"It's incredible!" he blustered. "Unconscionable, really!" He stole a look at Lambert and Weyers, who were
sitting backward on bridge chairs. "Bad enough my own
men attacked fellow soldiers, but now we're spying on
each other!" His eyes shifted to a memorandum that lay
on a plain end table. "There's sabotage in our factories,
leaks in spy networks on the Continent, fifth columnists
everywhere—and the Secret Intelligence Service wastes
manpower watching *us*! It's obscene!"

Weyers and Lambert nodded in agreement. Sunk in a
plush wing chair, Colon sat still, staring at his knees.
Behind him, the team's English member, Sergeant Major
Kenneth Ogan, stood beside drawn drapes. His arms
were tightly folded, his lantern jaw rigid. Livingston
stood beside him. A shade over six feet, he wore a
sharply pressed captain's uniform and a rugged, com-
manding look.

Escott stopped his pacing and glowered at the seated
men.

"Needless to say, I'm most disappointed in you. Inspector Sweet and I give you a night's leave, to relax, and what do you do?''

"Just what we were supposed to do," Weyers rejoined. "We relaxed!"

"That'll be enough of that," Livingston cautioned.

Escott flushed. "What you *did*, Corporal, was start an altercation which resulted in one man nearly drowning, and another suffering a pair of broken ribs!"

"Don't forget Captain Thorpe's *goullions*," Lambert said under his breath.

"What was that?"

"Nothing, sir. I was thinking aloud."

"Thinking? That's a matter of opinion, Corporal. Your problem is that you think too little! At the Yard, if any of my men had acted so recklessly, I would have suspended him without . . ."

Before he could continue, the door opened and a man walked in. He was tall and lean with horn-rimmed eyeglasses and a bowler. "They're not going to reprimand us," he said. "Or watch us anymore."

The portly inspector pressed his palms to his eyes and sighed. "Thank the Good Lord."

Sweet shut the door and pulled off his hat. "Actually, that's exactly who you should thank. Lord Oliver Caldwell came over from Whitehall and sat down with us, with the Secret Intelligence Service, and with Military Intelligence. The long and the short of it is that SIS has agreed to stop spying on Force Five and trying to give us a black eye. In exchange, our superiors at MI have agreed not to put together any more special units."

"What! After what we accomplished in Algiers—"

The lanky William Sweet slipped off his trench coat. "No, Bertie, *because* of it. SIS understands that our unit is unique, created because a leak in their ranks compromised all of their operatives. But they're very protective of their territory, and now that the leak's been plugged, they don't want our success to spur the creation of similar teams."

Escott threw up his hands. "Madness. All the enemy has to do to win this war is to sit back and let us destroy ourselves!"

Livingston pulled over an armchair. "From what Inspector Sweet tells me, there's just as much infighting at Scotland Yard."

"Why do you think we were glad to be seconded to MI? With so much at stake, it seemed reasonable, dare I say *imperative*, that there would be nothing but cooperation between the branches. God, we are the most *idiotic* creatures on this planet. Even my *dogs* have the good sense to chase the fox and not each other." He looked at Lambert, Weyers, and Colon. "But if my Jack Russells can learn discipline, then by God so can you. And if balmy Algiers didn't do it, then maybe a few days somewhere less inviting *shall*!"

Weyers and Lambert exchanged uncomfortable glances as, trailing clouds of pipe smoke, Escott strode to an easel beside the console radio. He drew back a sheet of paper and picked up a pointer, tapping it several times on the map of western Russia. He took some delight in the fact that Lambert buried his face in a hand.

"For three months now, a massive German army has laid siege to Stalingrad—which is here, some nine hundred kilometers southeast of Moscow. The Germans went in with the notion of taking the Lower Volga to control both the oil traffic and access to Russia's industrial centers. But Hitler saw Stalingrad as a splendid prize, a city of a half million souls to be taken and enslaved, and diverted the Sixth Army under General Paulus and the Fourth Panzer Army for this purpose.

"Despite heavy losses, the Russian defenders have held. Unfortunately, now that winter has come, Hitler is impatient and Paulus is desperate. As a result, they are prepared to add a new leaf to an already thick book of

wartime atrocities.'' Escott stepped from the map, his
eyes on the floor. ''According to radio transmissions intercepted by an operative in Turkey, Berlin has already
shipped massive amounts of dichlorodiethyl sulfide to the
city.''

Sweet said, ''Mustard gas.''

''Quite—but it's worse than the stuff with which you
men may be familiar. We believe this is an experimental
batch, one which we know they've been working on at
Farben. It's far more concentrated and lethal. It literally
hangs in the air wherever it's released, possibly for days.
It'll burn the skin off anyone who comes in contact with
it, destroy the lungs of anyone who breathes it. It's dam-
nable, barbaric stuff.

''The point is,'' he continued, ''if we can prevent the
shipment, the Russians have a good chance of breaking
the siege and driving the Nazis from Russia.''

After the men took a moment to digest what they'd
been told, Livingston said, ''I assume there's a reason
the Russians can't handle this mission by themselves.''

''It's a question of manpower, really. Everyone who is
able—man, woman, and child—is busy trying to get supplies and ammunition to the defenders. These people
aren't trained saboteurs, and to divert the numbers that
would be necessary to attack the convoy would be catastrophic for Stalingrad.'' Escott paused. ''And there's
another reason. When this business with Hitler is eventually finished, Stalin and the Bolsheviks will still be the
same treacherous bunch they've always been. Whitehall
and Washington both agree that it would be *unwise* to
allow the gas to fall into their hands.''

''In short,'' Sweet said, ''Force Five is going to Stalingrad to save the city . . . and to make absolutely certain that the shipment from Berlin ends up on the bottom
of the Volga.''

''Any questions?'' Escott asked.

Lambert raised a hand. "Just how cold *is* it in Stalingrad during the winter?"

"Well below zero," Escott said. "Or to put it another way, does the word *tundra* mean anything to you, Corporal?"

It was well below freezing as Sweet, Escott, and the five Force Five team members stepped from a pair of sedans onto the small military airfield outside London. Strong winds tore across the tarmac, and Lambert pulled the collar of his parka tightly around his neck. He and Weyers went to the back of the car. With one hand, the big South African pulled his duffel bag and parachute from the trunk, while with the other he handed Lambert his gear.

"There's no doubt about it," Lambert said as they headed toward the waiting B-17. "When we get back, I'm going to insist that I be transferred to warm, sunny North Africa."

"Under Patton?" He swore in Afrikaans.

"Why not? He treated us very well—"

"We'd just blown up a German airfield. When that wore off, he would have treated us just like everyone else."

"Meaning?"

The two men stepped aside as Livingston, Colon, and Ogan collected their gear.

"While we were recuperating in Casablanca, I heard that the bugger raided a food locker and gave the steaks to his dogs, the beets to his men. I'd rather be on my own *anywhere* than serve under that kind of bastard."

Lambert squinted into the harsh wind. "Not me. I believe it's better to serve in heaven than to freeze *mon derriere!*"

Escott smiled as he stood to one side and eavesdropped. Despite the Frenchman's grievances, he, like the others, was not a man to shy from the rigors of war.

Each man had been selected for Force Five due to his survival skills, abilities that had been expanded by Sweet and Escott to include training in espionage and self-defense.

The inspectors had had a week to work with the men before shipping them to Algiers; ideally, they would have liked some time to prepare them for Stalingrad. The men spoke German, but no Russian; they had limited experience with naval vessels; and only Weyers had ever used a parachute. But the orders had come from Military Intelligence just the day before, and as it was, there had been barely enough time for Sweet, Escott, Livingston, and Ogan to work out the logistics of the mission—and get the SIS off their back.

Lambert and Weyers followed Colon, Ogan, and Livingston through the forward entry hatch under the plane. As Weyers, Sweet, and Escott climbed up, the pilot came from behind the cockpit armor plate.

"Captain Kane?" Escott asked.

The tall newcomer nodded once. He wore a faded flight jacket capped by an equally leathery face; a mop of gray hair atop his head underscored the weatherbeaten look. But he was smiling, and Escott seemed encouraged.

"Are you Inspector Escott?"

"I am."

They shook hands. "It's rather cramped up here, Inspector. Let's go to the back, shall we?"

Heading from the nose section, he led the men through the bomb bay into the fuselage. There, Escott introduced the others. The pilot shook their hands in turn.

"It's going to be quite a run," he said with enthusiasm, "a spot of excitement after all those boring flights over Germany, dodging antiaircraft fire, enemy fighters, and the like."

Escott grinned. "Vice-Marshal Park tells me you have a strange notion of what constitutes excitement."

Kane shrugged. "I enjoy flying and I enjoy hurting the Hun. And this mission—frankly, sir, it's going to be a challenge. I don't think the Almighty's winged angels *themselves* could get into and out of Latvia. The Germans *own* that region. And we have to do it twice!"

Escott forced a smile. The B-17G bomber had a range of 3,200 kilometers, which was barely enough for a one-way trip. The plan called for them to fly to Latvia, on the Baltic Sea, where Kane would refuel on a barren stretch of field nearly fifty kilometers east of the seaport capital of Riga. On the return trip, he would have to stop and refuel a second time. If the mission in Stalingrad wasn't dangerous enough, getting there promised to be even riskier.

Kane turned his wrinkled face to Livingston. "Make yourself at home, Lieutenant—as much as you're able." He pointed to the plain, gunmetal benches bolted to either side of the fuselage. "They shake like the blazes, and your bum'll go numb from the cold. The loo's in the back—the big iron drum with the lid but no seat—and if anyone needs a rest, the auxiliary crew member's seat'll be empty. It's forward, right next to the radio operator."

Livingston thanked him, after which they began stowing their gear beneath the benches.

"See you in a few days," Escott said as he shook Livingston's hand.

"*Peut-etre,*" Lambert said. "If I find someplace warm over there, I won't be leaving it."

"The cold will be good for you," Sweet said. "It'll toughen you up."

"For what, my next trip to the Arctic? I'm not going to like this, messieurs. Not at all."

Escott said gravely, "The cold should be your worst problem, Corporal."

Wishing the men well, the two inspectors departed. A crew member shut the door, and the four 9-cylinder, turbo-supercharged engines were started up; the plane rattled as promised, and Lambert pulled his collar over his ears to muffle the drone.

"At least there's one thing to be thankful for, *mes amis*."

"What's that?" Weyers asked.

"At least the pilot's enthusiastic. We won't have to teach him *manners* when we get back."

Chapter Two

His eyes shut, Sergeant Major Ogan was nestled between a portable oxygen bottle, which was lashed to the wall, and a 12.7mm Browning M2 machine gun, which sat on a pole to his left and faced a shuttered, rectangular slot.

Though it was early, just six in the evening, he was exhausted; the combination of the droning and the vibration of the fuselage relaxed him. As soon as they were airborne, he drifted asleep. The only time he woke was when the bomber hit turbulence. His chest was still bandaged from the wounds he'd received in North Africa, and though they'd been less severe than bloody, they stung whenever he made any jerks or sudden, twisting motions.

During those periods when he was awake, Ogan knew that what he was feeling was partly mental and physical exhaustion from the long hours of planning the mission to Stalingrad: working on a flight plan that would bring them into Riga under cover of midnight, and helping to arrange, with Sweet, for Russian partisans to meet them at the field, and for two more to meet them in Stalingrad.

But part of it too was emotional exhaustion. Ogan still

had difficulty accepting the fact that he'd been relieved
of the command of Force Five. He didn't resent Livingston for having been promoted to second lieutenant. If
anything, he respected Livingston more for having saved
both the team and the mission in Algiers; his own deci-
sions in North Africa had been too cautious, too inex-
perienced. But it had been a humiliating setback for the
handpicked British member of the team, the inspectors'
fair-haired boy. He was glad that, upon his return to En-
gland, his wife had been able to make a quick trip from
Coventry. Without her support, picking himself up and
dusting himself off would have been more than emotion-
ally draining. It would have been impossible.

Across from Ogan, Livingston opened his duffel bag
and retrieved the thin dossier Military Intelligence had
put together on the situation in Stalingrad, and on the
operatives they would be meeting there; there was also a
psychological profile of General Paulus. Beside him, Colon was reading a Human Torch comic book.

"You played football at Benning, didn't you?" Livingston asked.

"Yes, sir. And for four years at Duquesne."

"Tell me—what went through your mind when you
had to face a goal-line stand."

"A thinkin' question, huh?" The private bent down
the corner of the page, shut the magazine. "What happens, sir, is you stand there sayin' to yourself, 'The
crowd's expectin' us to be able to move the ball a couple
of yards.' So you start thinkin' about *their* expectations,
and that's usually enough to distract you and *stop* you
from doin' it."

"And when you're a defender?"

"Just the opposite. You take each down as it comes,
focus on every second, every inch. I always found it
easier to score from *our own* two- or three- or four-yard
line than to punch in from theirs."

Livingston nodded. "That's something Hitler doesn't understand."

"Football?"

"The psychology of winning."

Colon gave him a puzzled look. "The bucket-heads have done well enough, considerin' how Hitler's pushed 'em—"

"No argument. But what you just said makes sense. They're less concerned with winning than with living up to Hitler's expectations. That's a helluva distraction."

Colon nodded inconclusively, then returned to his comic book.

Livingston riffled through the papers, looking for the history of the conflict in Russia. He'd learned many things during six years of fighting—first with the Abraham Lincoln Brigade, against Franco in Spain, and then with the French resistance before Pearl Harbor. However, the most valuable lesson he'd learned was that ambition and ability alone are never enough to win a war. As even Colon understood, it takes a will that comes from somewhere inside.

He found the two-page summary of the invasion of Russia and began reading.

When the U.S. finally agreed to join the war, Hitler was already waging war on two very difficult fronts: against the British and against the Russians. Of the two, the Russian front was far more draining on men and matériel. The defenders had their entire eastern section to draw upon, and they simply replaced the hundreds of thousands of soldiers as they fell. When Germans died, their comrades were expected to fight that much harder.

Hoping to effect a swift victory against the Russians, Hitler regrouped. He sent the massive Army Group A and the Fourth Panzer Army into the Caucasus, to capture the oilfields, while ordering the powerful Army Group B to take and hold the River Don. Taking it, Army Group B was ordered to cross the river and head southeast, to Stalingrad—which produced nearly one-third of the tanks, guns, tractors, and other vehicles used by the Russians.

It was at this point, Livingston noted, that Hitler made a catastrophic error. Encouraged by the progress of Army Group A, he ordered the Fourth Panzer Army to leave the Caucasus Front and help the struggling Army Group B. Just shy of their goal, Army Group A found itself stretched too thin, and was stopped dead by the Russians.

Meanwhile, the Germans at Stalingrad underestimated the determination of the defenders not to lose the city that bore their leader's name. After months of bitter fighting, without a victory, Hitler ordered the city razed with artillery fire and Luftwaffe bombing raids. When the smoke cleared, General Paulus's Sixth Army encircled Stalingrad, expecting an easy victory. Instead, the fighting became even more vicious. It was hand-to-hand, measured in meters, as the Russians fought from bombed-out buildings, from hastily dug tunnels, and from behind heaps of rubble.

Finally, November came, and desperate to give Hitler Stalingrad as a Christmas present, Paulus took the unprecedented step of requesting the poison gas. In defiance of the rules of warfare set down in Geneva, Hitler agreed.

Livingston flipped past the statistics and maps, rereading the scant material about their two contacts. After parachuting in, they would link up with Masha Vlasov and her younger brothers Andrei and Leonid. The Russians were lifelong residents of Stalingrad, and were couriers in the underground lines that brought food and ammunition into the besieged city. MI knew little else about them, save that only Masha spoke English. Their father had been a theatrical impresario, and she had traveled widely with him throughout Europe. Resourceful and daring, she was one of the partisans most sought after by the Germans.

For the Germans to acknowledge that a woman was hurting them, Masha *had* to be exceptional. Livingston was looking forward to meeting her.

After going forward and reviewing the flight plan with Captain Kane and his navigator, Livingston, Lambert, Weyers, and radio operator Forbes Rathbone crowded into the transmitter room to play poker. Copilot Derek Abel joined them for several hands, winning them all, after which Lambert joined him in the cockpit for a smoke. Two hours later, at a few minutes past 11 P.M., Abel and Lambert came back to the small but warm transmitter room. The copilot informed them that they were flying over the Baltic Sea on their approach toward Riga.

"You might want to go back and buckle in," he said. "We'll be dropping fast from thirty-two thousand feet, and will soon be within range of enemy guns. If we're spotted, things could get bumpy."

Livingston thanked him, and as soon as they entered the fuselage, their breath froze.

"Definitely the Pacific Theater next time," Lambert said. He dropped onto the bench and pulled the belt across his chest. "I was talking to the copilot, and did you know, the Romans used to fete their soldiers before sending them into battle? What did we get? A night at a dockside tavern. Where were the women, the confetti?"

Weyers said, "Better you should ask where the Romans are."

Without looking up from his magazine, Colon answered, "I agree with Rotter. Gimme a few hours of sun and a dame instead of a bulkhead and a *cavallo* like you."

Weyers's wide mouth turned down. "Those things'll

make a man soft.'' The frown deepened. ''And what the hell did you just call me, ya runt? A cava*what*?''

Colon bristled, but before he could answer Livingston ordered the men to be quiet. Though they'd gone through the plan for Riga in London, Livingston asked Ogan—who had made the arrangements—to review the procedure again.

''Two small bonfires will be lit on the field by partisans,'' he said, ''and the plane will come down between them. An oil truck will be waiting, part of the stores the Russians hid in June of last year, when the Nazis came from East Prussia into Lithuania and Latvia. Lambert and Weyers, you'll man the Browning machine guns here''—he pointed to the weapons on either side of the fuselage—''while the rest of us take up positions outside, to watch the perimeter while the Russians pump the fuel.''

No one had any questions and, as the plane rocked and lurched, radio operator Rathbone poked his head from the transmitter room.

''Captain Kane says we're just about one hundred kilometers out of Riga, and about to go down through the clouds. Keep a sharp lookout.''

Livingston glanced at his watch. ''Eleven thirty-five. Right on time.''

There was a great deal of turbulence as he and Lambert slid back the metal doors and peered through the machine-gun ports on their respective sides. As soon as they penetrated the thick cloud cover, the searchlights of the port city were visible some thirty kilometers to the south. Their own lights doused, inside and out, Kane held to a course well north of Riga. Before descending farther, he waited until they were twenty kilometers east of the city, then doubled back.

The men looked out carefully. After they circled the area twice, the fires flared on Lambert's side of the plane.

"We've got them below," he said.

A moment later, the stocky Abel came back. "Lieutenant, the captain says there may be a problem."

"What kind of problem?"

"Well, we've circled the field once, and make it out to be roughly a thousand meters long. That's over a hundred meters more than we need to land—but some fifty less than we need to take off again."

"Shit."

"Precisely. Now just to play it safe, he suggests you lighten the aircraft while we refuel; about a thousand pounds should do it."

Livingston nodded, and as the big main wheels and tail wheel were lowered, the team scanned the fuselage for anything that could be taken out quickly. As soon as the huge aircraft thumped down, Weyers and Lambert swung the machine guns toward the ports while Livingston, Ogan, and Colon unfastened everything from the oxygen bottles to the fire extinguishers to the toilet lid.

After less than a minute, Rathbone looked in on them. "Excuse me, Lieutenant, but Captain Kane would like to see you."

Livingston looked up from the cover of the auxiliary direct current generator, which he was in the process of detaching. "What is it?"

"Well, sir, it would seem that there are no Russians and no gasoline truck."

Livingston hurried through the transmitter room and empty bomb bay. Rounding the navigator's bench, he dropped through the open hatchway. His feet smarted when they hit the hard ground. Ignoring the eye-tearing cold and propeller-driven winds, he went over to Kane. The captain stood with his hands on his hips, staring into the adjacent woods.

"Nothing?" Livingston asked.

"Not a peep, not even a bloody squirrel. And if they aren't out there, I'd say we're in a bit of a jam—and not just because of the petrol."

Livingston understood. "Someone lit those fires."

"Exactly."

Livingston went back and pulled himself halfway into the plane. "Lambert! Weyers! Keep a sharp lookout! This may be a setup!" He dropped back down.

Kane asked, "Was there supposed to be a signal of some sort?"

"Nothing. The whole idea was to get in and out as quickly as—"

Sharp reports and white streaks burst from the dark woods, and Lambert's Browning cracked to life. Kane and Livingston jumped behind the main wheel as enemy fire dug up chunks of earth less than a meter from their feet. The guns fell silent, and they peered into the woods on the starboard side. Above, Weyers sent a warning burst into the woods on the port side.

"They must want us alive," Livingston said, "or they'd have picked us off when we first stepped out."

Ogan and the navigator appeared in the open hatch. Ogan lowered his hands.

"Come on!"

"You first," Livingston said, giving Kane a push. The pilot ran for the hatch, bullets tearing up clods of earth as Ogan grabbed his arms. Looping his legs inside, Kane pulled himself up.

Ogan bent out again for the lieutenant. "Let's go, sir!"

When Lambert and Weyers set up covering fire, Livingston jumped around the landing gear and literally dove up into the hatch. Ogan caught his arms and pulled him up as bullets tore the cuffs of his pants and raked the outside of his left leg.

"Get us the hell out of here!" Livingston hollered as he and Ogan shut the hatch.

Bullets chewed at the sides of the aircraft as Kane

throttled up. Ogan helped Livingston back, the aircraft
turning before they even reached their seats. Livingston
fell onto the bench, and Ogan, kneeling beside him, examined his leg.

"Doesn't look serious—"

"Forget it," Livingston barked. "Is anyone on the tail
gun?"

"Colon."

"Then you get to the chin turret, Ken—just in case
they try to roll something in front of us."

Ogan saluted and hurried forward. Livingston hobbled
behind him and stood behind the copilot, leaning on the
cylindrical hydraulic accumulator for support.

As they taxied, Livingston saw flashes of white close
in from both sides of the field. Bullets scraped cometlike
smudges on the bulletproof windshield; behind him, the
sharp clanging was constant as gunfire riddled the fuselage.

Suddenly, a Waffenwagen bolted from the woods, its
20mm cannon blazing. The small armored vehicle raced
toward the aircraft, Ogan's return fire bouncing from its
iron shell; as the B-17 rushed by, there was a pop and
the plane listed to one side.

"They got the bloody landing gear," Kane said
through his teeth.

The copilot quickly adjusted the flaps to try to give
them additional lift as they raced ahead. The aircraft leveled, and with the trees at the far end of the field less
than one hundred meters away, Kane pulled back on the
controls.

"Get Ogan up here!" he yelled.

"Why?"

"The damn chin turret may not clear!"

Swearing, Livingston limped around the armor plate
and shouted down as the huge bomber nosed up. Kane
immediately put the plane into a steep climb, listening
as the tops of the trees slapped against the plane's un-

derbelly. He heard the grinding of metal, first below and
then behind him as they cleared the woods.

He exhaled loudly, and moments later, Livingston and
Ogan staggered into the cockpit. They were followed by
the navigator. Several charts were gathered in his arms.
The wind tore in from the ruptured nose section.

"How much did we lose?" Kane asked.

"The chin turret and cheek guns both," the navigator
answered, "along with the floor under my table. I saved
what I could."

"Good show." He patted him on the arm, then said
to Livingston, "You know, Lieutenant, we really do owe
the Jerries our thanks."

"For what?"

"For not letting us refuel. Even after ditching a half
ton, there isn't a way in hell we'd have done it with a
full tank of petrol."

Despite the cold, Livingston wiped sweat from his
brow. As in Algiers, it seemed as if Force Five was
cursed. Once again, from the very start, nothing was
going as planned.

Slumping against the hydraulic panel, the American
noticed a red light burning beside the pilot's left foot.
"What's that?"

Kane looked down. "Landing gear warning light. It
means the struts are stuck halfway between extended and
retracted."

"Can we fix it?"

"Not if the trees tore either of them out of alignment.
In any case, why bother? I'll be very much surprised if
there's anything left below the shock absorber. Whether
they're up or down makes very little difference."

Livingston had to admit that that made sense.

"And now, sir," Kane went on, "it's up to you.
We've got enough fuel to turn round, or else go most
of the way to Stalingrad. If we go home, the plane can
be saved."

"And if we don't, Stalingrad can be saved. From my point of view, there isn't much choice."

Kane looked from his copilot to the navigator. "Yes, well—the crew and I are up for a little adventure. Southeast, then?"

"Southeast," Livingston said, smiling and then heading back to take care of his leg.

Chapter Three

"**H**ow do you think they found out about us?"

Livingston's question, though expected, caused Lambert to shift uncomfortably, and Weyers to look away. The landing had been Ogan's responsibility. As with those parts of the Algerian mission that had gone wrong, he was the one who had to answer for it.

"Ken? Was there any possible way the Germans could have intercepted your communiqués?"

"Possible, but unlikely. We broadcast on a frequency that no one uses or monitors any longer."

"Then what happened?"

"If I had to guess, I'd say the Germans had no idea we were coming. The remnants of the Russian Eighth Army have been in the hills since Hitler invaded. Rather than send troops after them, the enemy probably waited for them to show themselves, to attempt something bolder than cutting telephone lines and sabotaging tanks and planes."

Livingston stretched his bandaged leg along the bench. "And this was it."

"That's my feeling," Ogan said.

"Then chances are good they don't know about Stalingrad. They must've captured those poor bastards right after they lit the fires.''

"Most likely."

Lambert said, "If I may, Lieutenant—what are our plans now for Stalingrad? Do we jump, or are we really going to try to land in this wreck?"

"Weyers, you've done both. What do you say?"

The big man leaned on the machine gun. "Me? Call me practical, but I'd put my faith in a working parachute before I'd trust a plane without landing gear."

Livingston nodded. "That's how I feel. We can arrange to meet Kane and the others after they set down. What's important is that *we* get as close to the target area as possible, and in one piece." He looked at his watch. "We've got six hours. I suggest everyone try to get some shut-eye, since I doubt we'll be getting much rest once we land."

Colon, Weyers, and Lambert curled up beside their machine guns, and Ogan pulled a small book from his jacket pocket. Pouring them both some coffee the radio operator made, Livingston sat beside him.

"What're you reading?"

Ogan turned the cover around. "A Russian-English dictionary. Just in case."

Livingston smiled. "Glad someone around here's thinking ahead."

"For all the good it does. I want you to know, Lieutenant, I'm sorry about what happened back there."

"No reason to—"

"But there *is*. The *entire* mission was placed in jeopardy because we failed to ask ourselves, 'What if?' "

"And if you had? What could we possibly have done any differently?"

"We might have planned a straight-through flight to Stalingrad and tried to refuel there, or we could have had a fighter go into Riga first. A mustang could have made the trip—"

"And been snookered, just like we were. Ken, we only had thirty-six hours to pull this together. Besides, you heard what Kane said. What happened was a blessing in disguise."

"Not for the Russians."

Livingston's voice was somber. "No, not for them. But like it or not, that's the price of doing business. We're risking our necks to save Russians; I can't hurt for the couple of Russians who let down their guard and got their necks wrung."

Ogan returned to his book.

"You're not convinced."

"No, sir. I hate to sound like a tyro, but I don't think I'll ever be able to just shrug it off when someone dies because of something I did or didn't do."

Livingston stretched out his bandaged leg, pulled his cap over his eyes. "Well, maybe a little compassion is good for the team, just as long as it doesn't interfere with one thing."

"What's that?"

He lifted the edge of his cap. "Killing Nazis. As long as you don't hurt for *them*, I can live with the rest of it."

The lieutenant could feel Ogan's eyes on him as he settled back into the seat. But that didn't bother him. He himself had felt righteous, once; it had died the first time he'd had to execute a saboteur in Spain, a young woman. And it had been buried for good when he saw an enemy chaplain pick up a bayonet and drive it into a man's back for raping a nun. Sometimes it took a few battles, but in the end, war turned everyone into a survivor.

"Lieutenant. *Lieutenant!*"

Livingston's nose was numb. That was the first thing of which he was aware. The second was that perspiration had literally frozen his fatigues around his body. He barely felt Lambert's prodding.

"What time is it?"

"Just after four, sir—but we've got a problem. Captain Kane asked to see you, *tout de suite*."

Livingston was instantly alert. He jumped up, his leg smarting, his clothing cracking loudly as he hurried to the cockpit. He stood in silence as Kane and the navigator shouted numbers to each other over the drone of the engines.

"The situation is this," Kane said when they were finished. "We're nearly three hundred kilometers northwest of Stalingrad, and I don't think I can stay aloft for more than another hundred kilometers. How long will your people in Stalingrad wait for you?"

Livingston turned around. "Ogan! Up front on the double!"

The sergeant major came quickly, and Livingston repeated Kane's question. Ogan shook his head.

"I'm not sure; we kept communications to a minimum. If they don't think we're coming, my guess is they'll decide to go after the cargo themselves."

"That's just great."

Kane said, "Well, all isn't quite that hopeless, Lieutenant." He nodded toward a map. "See here. Mr. Poole tells me there's a sizable village on our route. Urisomething."

The navigator plucked a pencil from behind his ear. "Uryupinsk," he said, circling it on the map.

"Right. We'll reach it in just a few minutes. Now then, you can probably find a vehicle of some sort there and make your way south. What's more, the charts say there's nothing but hills and fields for nearly a hundred kilometers in all directions. I can ditch this lady somewhere along the way and, hopefully, we can all link up."

"And if we stay with you, how close can you get us to Stalingrad?"

"Probably two hundred kilometers. At best, one-fifty, if God sees fit to give us a tail wind."

Livingston weighed the options, then turned. "Come on, Ken. We're moving out."

Gathering their gear, the men put on the German uniforms they'd been provided with, Lambert shivering violently as he changed. He felt better when he'd donned his animal skin fur coat, field gray fur cap, and parachute. Weyers checked each man's harness before they headed to the bomb bay. They waited there while Poole guided Captain Kane toward their destination.

Lambert looked at his thick arms. "I feel like the Monster of Frankenstein in this. I can hardly move."

"It's better than freezing," Weyers said. He looked at Livingston. "If I were you, sir, I'd take the landing on my good leg and roll to that side. You've got enough padding. Otherwise, if you hit with both legs, you may pop your bandages."

Livingston thanked him.

"Also," the South African said, "it's going to be cold out there, so I suggest we cover our faces." He looked at Lambert. "That includes keeping your mouth shut so your tongue doesn't freeze."

"That can happen?" the Frenchman asked.

"Tongue, eyes, nose—anything damp or exposed is going to take a hell of a lashing."

The copilot gave the men rags, Lambert stuffing extra padding into the front of his pants.

The plane had dropped steadily from its service ceiling of 10,800 meters until it was just 1,100 meters high. At four-forty, Copilot Abel came through the cockpit door.

"We're nearly over the village. Best be getting to the hatchway."

The men squeezed through the cabin into the nose section, where the copilot had pushed aside the remains of the bomb sight, navigator's table, and cheek-gun ammunition box. The men gathered around the wide, jagged gash in the hull, all that was left of the forward hatch. The wind was bone chilling and fierce.

Lambert swore. "Someone shoot me *now*!"

The copilot stood back. "I'll give you the signal! You've got about"—he looked at the captain, who nodded—"forty-five seconds."

Lambert tried to wrap his arms around his chest, but the coat was too stiff. Colon crouched, Weyers moved slowly from foot to foot, and Ogan rubbed his gloved hands. Livingston watched the copilot.

"Thirty seconds."

Livingston looked through the hole. Below, the dark terrain was broken by the occasional light of a home, a car, or a fire.

Soldiers keeping warm, he guessed. He wondered what they thought his plane might be.

"Twenty seconds!"

Livingston looked at the men. "I'll go first, then Weyers, Lambert, Ogan, and Colon."

"Ten!"

Weyers yelled through the cloth covering, "Don't hesitate! Go out, turn facedown, count to ten, then pull the cord. And remember to *give* when you hit. Don't try to *stay* on your feet!"

"Five!"

Livingston sat on the lip of torn metal as Weyers gave them a few more suggestions. He only half heard them.

"Three!"

He had to push out, just enough so his chute would clear the rim.

"Two!"

Weyers squatted beside him, ready to take his place the instant Livingston jumped.

"One—"

Livingston's heart punched hard and fast against his throat.

"Go!"

The lieutenant arched his body and slid from the rim, pushing back as he went through. He cleared the hatch and found himself on his back.

It was a sensation like nothing he'd ever felt, but it was also not at all what he'd been expecting. Instead of the stomach-turning drop he'd been anticipating, he felt as if he was floating on a loud, choppy sea. The air actually seemed solid, and it tore past him with fury that made him feel as though he were lying still. He couldn't see the B-17, nor, in the dark, did he see the other men; the droning of the plane was quickly swallowed up by the deafening roar of the wind.

So caught up in the jump was he that Livingston had to force himself to concentrate on what he was supposed to be doing. Remembering what Weyers had said, he drew in his arms and legs and did a slow, awkward somersault until he was facedown. He realized, then, that he'd forgotten to count. Because it had to have been at least ten seconds since he'd jumped—he couldn't be sure; time didn't seem to exist in this dark, dreamlike world—Livingston reached to his side and tugged on the ripcord.

Reality returned with a jolt.

He didn't see the parachute, but he heard and felt it. The fabric sounded like a flock of birds scared into flight, and even through his thick coat, the jerk of the harness was sufficient to kick the air from his chest. As he descended feetfirst, twisting slightly in the wind, the air was no longer so loud, nor so thick. *Now* he felt like he was falling.

He looked to his right, caught a glimpse of another chute some twenty meters off. Then he looked down. He recalled Weyers having said that if they saw trees, they should pull hard on the side of the chute toward them, so they'd drift in the opposite direction. But, as far as Livingston could see, there was nothing but open field below. He thought he saw a home or a farmhouse off in the distance, but it was too dark to be certain. He glanced down again, his eyes barely open to protect them from the wind.

Then he was on the ground, before he knew it. One moment it was barely visible, a bleak stretch of dirt mounds and withered grass; the next moment it was rushing up at him, like a bull he'd once crossed in Spain. He pulled in his injured leg slightly, took the landing on his right leg—

He was only on the leg for an instant. As soon as he touched down, the parachute dragged him down, onto his face. He had the wind knocked from him again, and it was several seconds before he could gather up the shroud lines, curl onto his back, bring his heels around, and dig in to stop. The chute drew him to his feet again, and he limped forward as he struggled to pinch the quick-release hook. When the chute finally came off, he scooped up the lines and hauled in the deflated canopy.

He turned, saw Weyers land with precision just ten meters away, followed by Colon. Both men undid their chutes without difficulty.

Weyers jogged over. "I've never seen it done quite like you did it, sir."

"Save it for your memoirs," he said, more disgusted with his own ineptitude than with Weyers's insubordination. He finished bunching up the canopy and handed it to Weyers. "Bury 'em. I'm going to see about the others."

"I saw Ogan come down about fifty meters past Colon. But I didn't see Lambert at all."

"It figures."

Livingston hurried off. As he'd suspected, they'd landed in a farm. The fields appeared to have been stripped clean, probably by the Germans before winter. He stopped to make sure that Colon and Ogan were all right, and determining that neither of them had seen Lambert, Livingston pulled off his glove, pulled the Luger in his pocket, and headed toward the house.

He circled wide, moving with extreme caution, then froze when he noticed a light on the second floor go on. He stood stone-still, and as the horizon began to shade from black to dark blue, he realized that this was probably when these people got up. He continued searching, his pace quickened.

As soon as he was on the other side of the house, he saw a small barn—and Lambert. His chute was draped from the dome of the silo, the Frenchman dangling facefront beneath it. He was trying to reach back and climb the shroud lines, but his bulky coat made it impossible for him to turn or lift his arms.

The silo was roughly five meters high, and were he to fall from that height, Lambert would certainly break his leg. Livingston thought of going back and gathering the other parachutes, to try to form a cushion. But the sun was rising quickly, and there wasn't time. Propelled by an oath, Livingston hurried toward him.

When Lambert saw him, he stopped struggling and shrugged. Livingston motioned for him to be quiet, then went around to the other side. A ladder was attached to the lower bin, and it rose to the dome; the uppermost rung was about two meters from the side of the chute. Somehow, he would have to find a way to reach it.

He looked around, heard a horse whinny in its stall.

There were animals. That meant there must also be hay.

Rushing inside, he felt along the dark walls until he found what he needed: a pitchfork. Grabbing it from the hook, he raced back outside.

The horizon was already a band of blue-green as he started up the ladder. He climbed quickly, and, reaching the top, latched the hook of Lambert's harness to the top rung of the pitchfork, a thin metal bar. Leaning to the side, his foot braced on the joint where the dome met the lower bin, he snagged the lines almost at once. Then he whispered loudly to Lambert.

"When I start to pull, you walk yourself around, on your heels. Just take it slow, understand? If the lines come loose, we're screwed."

"Oui!"

Holding the pitchfork so the tines were nearly upright, he slowly began to draw them around. Lambert's boots clumped and echoed through the empty silo, and Livingston prayed that no one in the house heard them. All the while, he had an odd sense of déjà vu, feeling the way he did when, as a child, he'd use a stick to try and work a kite free from the trees in Central Park. He tried not to think of just how *many* kites he'd lost that way. . . .

Livingston's arm began to cramp, and he relieved the strain by bracing the handle of the pitchfork on his knee. Finally, the shroud lines were within reach and, tossing the pitchfork to the ground, Livingston grabbed them. He looped them around the ladder and around his arm as Lambert inched over. He stole another look at the horizon, which was now a dull yellow.

It took just a few seconds more for Lambert to reach the ladder. The instant he grabbed it, Livingston undid the harness lest a gust of wind pull him off.

"You won't believe it," Lambert said through his muffler. "This only happened because I tried to *avoid* landing on the barn!"

Lambert was chattering from the cold and, having taken off his gloves, his hands were nearly frostbitten. After they were down, Livingston handed him his own gloves, then bundled up the parachute and stuffed it behind a skimpy bale of hay in the barn. They started toward the field; as they passed the house, a shotgun blast disrupted the still morning.

"Ahdyeen meenootah pahzhahloostah!"

Livingston looked toward the house, at the silhouette of a man standing in the doorway. He had no idea what the Russian had said; all he knew was that before he could reach his Luger, either Lambert or he would be dead.

Chapter Four

As the three men stood there, each waiting to see what the other would do, a second shot echoed across the field. This one came from the west; the short, stocky farmer turned, startled, and a second shot exploded, dislodging a small rock less than a meter from his foot.

He looked out and saw three men standing midway across the field, weapons drawn. Licking his lips, the farmer dropped his shotgun and raised his hands.

"Smart move," Livingston said, and came forward. A look of surprise crossed the Russian's round face.

Ogan, Weyers, and Colon arrived moments later.

"Whose shot was that?" Livingston asked.

"Mine," Ogan said. "We came to check—couldn't imagine what was taking so long."

The lieutenant nodded. "Glad you did."

"*I'm* just glad the Russian bugger didn't fire again," Weyers said. "If it were me instead of the sergeant calling the shots, I'd have nailed him."

"And not only would you have killed a potential ally," Ogan said, "but you'd have shot a man who apparently meant us no harm."

"How do you know that?"

"Because what he yelled was, 'A moment, please.' Quite deferential."

"Deference—with a shotgun," Weyers said. "I'm not comforted."

The Russian, a man Livingston guessed to be in his early fifties, still seemed confused. He looked from the men's military-issue coats to their faces. *"Nyehmyetski?"* he asked. *"Nyehmyetski?"*

Ogan said, "I believe, Lieutenant, he's asking if we're German."

Livingston rubbed his chin. "Answer him."

"Nyet," Ogan said. *"Yah Angliski."*

The man's gloomy features seemed to catch a piece of the rising sun. *"Da?"* The Russian was suddenly unable to contain himself. Pulling Ogan by the hand, he led him toward the house, motioning for the others to follow. They turned to Livingston.

"I smell a fire inside," Lambert said, "and I'll bet there's something warm cooking on it."

"We can't afford to stop now," Livingston said. "Ken, find out if he's got a car or a truck somewhere."

Ogan stopped the man, and managed to make himself understood. With obvious regret, the farmer said he had no vehicles, only two horses.

"Ask him how far it is to Uryupinsk."

"Uryupinsk?" The Russian regarded Livingston. He pointed past the house, held up two fingers. *"Dvah* kilometers."

Livingston looked at his watch. It was nearly six o'clock. They were already late, and needed to find out where they could get a car. Reluctantly, he motioned for the men to follow the Russian inside.

The farmer's name was Alexandre Mekhlis, and his wife was Caterina. They served the men bread and eggs. From what Ogan could gather, their home and barn had been used to billet German soldiers during their summer advance. Before leaving, the enemy took most of the crops and destroyed what they couldn't carry, so the Russian troops wouldn't have it. The couple survived on what little their cows and chickens were able to produce. Livingston felt guilty about accepting their hospitality.

"The only reason they left the animals," Ogan said, after checking several words in his dictionary, "is because they want to use them to feed their armies later."

"When they retreat," Colon vowed.

Weyers grumbled, "Nix. The Jerries'll be eating lead before that."

Though he was bitter when he spoke about the German invaders, their host literally thumped his chest with pride when he talked about his *"chyeetiryeh sihn"* who had gone off to fight them. As far as Ogan could determine, the farmers hadn't heard from their four boys in over a year.

As Caterina offered the men helpings of porridge, Livingston glanced at his watch. Only a half hour had passed, though it seemed much longer; the stone hearth was warm, and the thaw, as well as the meal, had had an almost narcotic effect. But the convoy was due in just over thirty-six hours, and guilt began to gnaw at him.

He rose. *"Spasibo,"* he said, having picked up the word from the conversation. "Thank you."

Their host stood, bowed. *"Nyeh zha shto."*

"I guess that means we're leavin'," Weyers said, and he literally had to pull Lambert from the fire.

Alexandre offered to ride into town with one of them to see about a car. He said there were rarely any Germans around anymore, and that, if he asked the right people, it might be possible to buy, borrow, or even steal some kind of transportation. He added that he had a good idea where they could start their search.

As he was the only one who had ever ridden bareback, Lambert volunteered to accompany him. That suited him

more than walking with the others, and as the Frenchman reined one of the farmer's old mares onto the road,
and felt the warmth of the rising sun, he shuddered with
gratitude. However, his joy was short-lived, as the galloping of the horse sent frigid air riding up his pant legs
and coat. That had never happened to him in the Legion,
and he realized, bitterly, that he'd never ridden anywhere
that wasn't in or near a desert. Nor had the sands of
Timimoun or Idehan been as lumpy as the road to Uryupinsk. His buttocks slammed repeatedly onto the animal's bony back, and by the time they reached the village
at six, after nearly an hour, Lambert envied those who
were merely suffering from hypothermia.

Uryupinsk was as small and impoverished as Lambert
had imagined. Several shops were shuttered: the tailor,
the blacksmith, and the baker. After they'd dismounted,
Alexandre used vivid sign language to explain that the
first two shopowners had been taken by the German infantry to accompany them to the front; the baker had
been executed when he struck a soldier for stealing his
goods.

They stopped on the stoop of a small shop that ser-
viced the local farmers. Alexandre drove the side of his
fist against the wooden door; within moments, the shut-
ters creaked open on the second floor. Lambert saw fear
in the face above; when the man saw the Frenchman's
German uniform, the color evaporated from his ruddy
cheeks. Then he noticed Alexandre, and the trepidation
turned to confusion. The farmer called for him to come
down, and a minute later, a bolt was thrown and the
front door opened.

"Alexandre." The bearded proprietor clasped the
farmer's hand and shook it tentatively. "Come in, come
in." Alexandre entered and Lambert followed him. The
bearded man's eyes followed the Frenchman closely.

"It's good to see you, Mikhail!" Alexandre said.

"Is it?"

"Yes. You'll never believe what happened last night."

"Tell me it rained gold on your property. Tell me that you have come to your friend Mikhail to *spend* some of it."

The farmer beamed. "It rained, yes—not gold, but something nearly as good."

Mikhail's eyes finally shifted to Alexandre. "Does it have to do with this . . . Nazi?"

"Nazi? He is no more a Nazi than I am."

Alexandre launched into an explanation and, having no idea what the men were saying, Lambert walked around. There were several plows and stacks of pitchforks, hoes, and other implements. But there was no feed, and where the large barrels must have stood, there were now only dark, discolored circles on the floor. He assumed the Nazis had taken it for their horses.

After a short, excited explanation, followed by a brief discussion, the men came over to Lambert. Alexandre said something slowly—as though that alone would magically help the Frenchman to understand Russian—of which the only word that made any sense was *"mashinyu."*

"Le machine?" he asked in French. *"La voiture?"*

The Russians looked at each other and shrugged. Grabbing Lambert's hand, Mikhail led him out back.

There, in an alley, was a battered pickup truck. The windows were all shattered, and the seats were ripped up, but the tires were intact. Wondering why the Germans hadn't taken this as well, Lambert went over to examine the engine. As he passed the driver's side, he noticed a black medical kit on the front seat. Presumably, Mikhail was also a part-time veterinarian; which meant, as it did in many small villages in North Africa as well, that the man was also the local physician. Obviously, the Germans didn't know that or they might have taken him with the blacksmith and the tailor.

As soon as he raised the hood, Lambert saw why the truck was still there. A thick layer of frost coated the

battery, and the fan belt was stiff as iron. It would need
some work, more than the invaders had been willing to
spend. However, nothing he saw seemed beyond repair.

"*Le feu,*" he said to their blank expressions. "Fire!"

"*Pazhar?*" Mikhail asked, striking an imaginary
match.

"*Oui, pazhar,*" Lambert said as he pulled off his
gloves and began disconnecting the battery.

It was nearly 7 A.M. when, 150 kilometers to the
northwest, Captain Kane's aircraft ran out of fuel. The
pilot managed to guide the plane over a forest toward a
stretch of ice, and, dropping from a height of twenty
meters, the B-17 went skidding across the frozen lake.
Just two of its huge propellers had still been turning, and
upon impact, they shut down in a spray of ice and shattered metal. The force of the impact threw the aircraft
into a swift, dizzying circle. Disoriented, the men were
unaware that the awful grinding all around them was
more just the belly of the plane dragging across the ice.
The half-extended landing struts dug deep troughs in the
gleaming expanse, causing it to crack; the instant the
aircraft stopped moving horizontally, it sloped vertically,
the nose rising as water flooded through rents in the rear
of the fuselage. Within moments the plane was nearly
perpendicular to the ice, only the wings sprawling across
unbroken sections of ice preventing it from going under.

The radio operator and the navigator—who had been
sitting in the extra seat beside him—were caught in the
icy flood as the transmitter room went under. Though
dazed from the crash landing, and blinded by the thick
clouds of steam pouring in from the cooling engines,
Kane could hear their screams. But only for a moment.
Soon, there was only the roar of the rushing water and
the creaking of tortured metal.

"Abel! Abel, are you all right?"

There was no answer, and Kane took a moment to get

his bearings. He lay flat on his back in his seat, pinned by the armor plate that had become dislodged. Undoing his seat harness, he pushed against the metal slab.

He could see nothing to his right, and squirmed lower into the seat to try to get around the plate.

"*Abel*—are you in one piece?"

The captain heard a moan and, wriggling from the seat, felt about for the copilot's chair. He found it lying on its side, against the fuse panel beside the bomb-bay door. The force of the impact had ripped it from the two struts that held it to the floor.

The plane shuddered and dropped slightly, as the ice began to give beneath the starboard wing. Kane undid his companion's seat belt and checked his wounds. Abel's right arm was twisted behind him with a compound fracture; debris had raised deep gashes in his scalp, forehead, and shoulder. Kane suspected that he had suffered a concussion.

"Afraid I didn't do too well on this one," the pilot apologized. "I just didn't expect to lose those port screws before we touched down."

As he glanced down through the misty bomb bay, Kane saw the water rising quickly. The only way out was forward, through the hatch. Lifting Abel over his shoulder, the pilot used the bent seat struts as grips and climbed into the nose. He reached the torn hatchway and, Abel draped across his shoulder, jumped down. Laying the wounded man down and grabbing his collar, Kane dragged him behind as he started across the ice.

As he trudged away, the plane continued to shift and settle. Below him, the surface of the ice rippled ominously, and shifting the copilot onto his shoulder, Kane summoned his last reserves of strength and ran to the frozen shore.

Reaching it, he fell to his knees and lay the copilot on his back.

"Captain—" Abel moaned.

"I'm here."

"Where . . . are we?"

"On dry land. Just need to do a few repairs on the old flesh and bones, and then we can set out." Kane gave him a reassuring pat on the thigh. "Don't you worry, chum. Everything's just ducky."

After taking a moment to catch his breath, the captain rose. He glanced around. The first order of business was to make a splint for Abel, after which he'd have to find a warm place to leave him while he went to the main road to wait for Livingston.

In search of a suitably strong branch, Kane walked into the sparse wood beside the lake. He found, instead, a German patrol.

By the time Livingston and his men reached Uryupinsk at nine, Lambert had suspended the battery between a pair of hoe handles and was warming it over a fire. He had already used a hot, damp cloth to massage the ice from the fan belt, and was busy cleaning the battery connections.

"You missed all the fun!" the Frenchman said from under the hood. "The horse was terrible, and then the three of us were acting like deaf mutes, trying to understand one another, until *mon ami* Mikhail thought to try German."

"Who knew you'd also speak the part?" the merchant said.

"Now we're making good progress, and if the battery dries out, everything else should be fine."

Weyers surveyed the scene. "If you Frenchies are so damn resourceful, how the hell did Hitler ever knock you off?"

Lambert said matter-of-factly, "I wasn't there, *naturellement*."

Weyers took what little oil and gas Mikhail had and used it to fill the tanks, while Colon helped Lambert with the engine. Finally, after an additional half hour's work, and several heart-stopping tries, the engine did turn over.

Livingston and Ogan came outside, the sergeant major folding a black-and-white map Mikhail had provided. While the men piled into the truck, the lieutenant pressed a small wad of rubles into Mikhail's hand.

"We were given these in the event of an emergency. I want you to have them."

The Russian smiled and handed the money back. "Thank you, but no. I have nothing to spend it on, and besides, you may need it yet." He said emphatically, "*Help* our people, and that will be payment enough."

Thanking him, Livingston climbed into the passenger's seat. Colon was already behind the wheel, and the other men sat in the open back.

"You know where you're going?" the lieutenant asked.

Colon looked back through the shattered rear windshield. "Yes, sir. Out the alley, then left until sunset."

Livingston folded away the map. "Believe it or not, that's about the size of it. Let's move it out."

With that, Colon shifted into reverse and backed through the alley beside the shop, onto the hard, dirt road.

The *oberleutnant* in charge of the small mounted reconnaissance detachment looked from the pilot to the moaning copilot. Kane was sitting on the ground, trembling from the cold, his hands tied behind him; Abel lay sprawled beside him on the hard ground. In the distance, two soldiers were bravely crossing the chunks of cracked ice, headed toward the plane.

"We can help your friend," the ascetic young German said. "Tell us why you are here and we will take him to the medic. It is eight o'clock . . . we can have him there in less than an hour."

"My name is Robert F. Kane, Captain, Royal Air Force, serial number—"

The *oberleutnant* slapped him with the back of his

hand. "Idiot! Don't you realize that you will tell us, eventually, everything we wish to know?"

Kane's eyes grew hard. "My name is Robert F. Kane, Captain, Royal—"

The officer slapped him again, then drew the ten-inch dagger that hung from the belt beneath his greatcoat. The pilot rose defiantly, but the *oberleutnant* pushed him back down. The German grabbed a handful of the copilot's blood-matted hair and, raising his head, put the side of the blade to his throat.

"I'll ask you one more time, *Herr Kapitan*. Why are you here?"

Kane looked from the officer to his friend. He suffered a moment of doubt; he'd been with Abel for years. Yet he knew how scarce supplies were on the Russian front, and suspected they'd be executed in any case. There was no sense jeopardizing the mission. Swallowing hard, he said, "My name is Robert F. Kane, Captain—"

Teeth clenched, the officer dragged the dagger across Abel's flesh. Blood spilled out in a sheet, flooding onto the snow. The *oberleutnant* stepped over the corpse and towered over Kane.

"One last time, *Englander*. Why are you here?"

Kane looked at his dead friend. "Afraid we didn't do too well on this one," he said softly. Drawing a deep breath, he repeated his name and rank once again. Snarling, the officer kicked him onto his back and drove the dagger through the base of his neck.

A few minutes later, the two men from the plane returned with an armful of charts. On one, a small village had been circled.

"Uryupinsk?" the *oberleutnant* said under his breath. Puzzled, he summoned the *funkmeister* in charge of the field radio and contacted headquarters in Frolovo.

The ride was bumpy, but the truck held up as Livingston and his men traveled along the wide, dirt road that ran southeast from the city. It was the major road leading to Stalingrad, and though it was possible they might encounter German forces along the way, that was a chance they'd have to take. Not only was this the quickest route, but also, according to the map, the road would take them through several small towns where they might be able to purchase gasoline—assuming the Germans had left any behind. Livingston wasn't optimistic. The first two towns through which they passed had no gas, and the last had no people at all, just fire-gutted buildings and fresh graves. That was the price, Alexandre had said, of refusing to provide supplies to the enemy.

By late morning, Livingston was beginning to experience a vague sense of dispiritedness—largely, he felt, because they hadn't yet found the B-17. As the fuel gauge edged toward empty, Livingston would have welcomed Captain Kane's optimism.

The men rotated every hour, with someone else taking the passenger seat; having demonstrated in Algiers that he was the best driver on the team, Colon remained behind the wheel.

It was Livingston, Lambert, and Weyers who were in the back when, shortly after eleven o'clock, a German cavalry unit came toward them from over a rise. The soldiers in the front were pointing broadly in their direction.

Livingston counted the men as they neared. There were fourteen in all, and they were approaching at a gallop—obviously with a destination in mind. Quite possibly, it had nothing to do with them. Then again . . .

He quickly thought it through. Maybe someone had seen them in Uryupinsk or one of the other villages. Maybe someone in Riga had guessed where they were headed. Maybe the B-17 had come down smack in the middle of General Paulus's camp.

Weyers stuck his gloved hands under his armpits to try

to warm them. "They look like they mean to have a chat, Lieutenant. What do we tell them?"

Livingston looked around. There was an open field to one side, and a wide stream to the other.

Nowhere to run.

Livingston said, "We haven't got papers, permits, or a story that'll make us sound even remotely legit." He leaned in through the shattered back window. "Private Colon—if they stop, tear through them."

A smile touched the soldier's lips.

Weyers drove a fist into his palm. "That's *my* kind of social intercourse."

"Lieutenant," Ogan said, "you realize that if we hit any of the animals flush-on, it could crush us."

"I'm aware of that. But if we don't panic them, and one of those men gets to his submachine gun, it'll do a lot more damage."

Livingston and the others unpocketed their pistols, then watched tensely as the troops neared. The nearest inhabited village was roughly twenty kilometers behind them. The lieutenant realized that there was no way these soldiers were galloping toward it; the horses would never last. The Germans were coming for them, a conviction underscored when, still two hundred meters away, the approaching *unterwachtmeister* held up his hand.

"It's us, all right," Lambert said.

Livingston lay on his belly between the men, facing back. "You two take the flanks, I'll cover the rear. Colon! If we manage to break through, keep us in range. We can't afford to leave any of them alive to report ahead."

The private threw him a two-fingered salute, then shifted into first. He pressed down on the gas and the truck surged ahead.

There was a long moment when the cavalrymen seemed frozen. Then, just before impact, the sergeant reined his horse to the side. The others followed and the truck sped through, half of the soldiers on either side falling in the first volley. But one soldier held his ground, tightly reining the horse with one hand, while firing at Colon with the other. The private ducked and the truck flew against the animal, which had reared in panic. The horse pirouetted, throwing the cavalryman through the broken windshield. The car hit the animal and swerved, skidding down the incline, spinning, and ending up sitting backward in the icy stream.

Livingston was sprawled in the back of the truck, though he'd lost his gun. He saw Weyers in the river, on his knees and shaking his head, but he couldn't see Lambert. Nor was there any time to search. There were shouts from the road as the *unterwachtmeister* tried to regroup his men; he heard someone moving in the cab but didn't know if it was one of his men or the soldier. The answer came in the form of a muffled gunshot, after which Colon sat up.

"Goddamn Kraut ball-buster!"

"How's Ogan?" Livingston asked.

The passenger's door opened and the Englishman slid out. "I'm all right." Suddenly, he bolted upright. "Christ! *Lambert!*"

Livingston looked over as Ogan rushed up the gentle incline. He saw the Frenchman lying unconscious beside the road, a clear target for the Germans who were dismounting and taking up positions on the opposite side.

"Weyers—Colon—cover him!"

Colon aimed through the windshield, while Weyers scrambled along the riverbank, swearing and trying to find his weapon. Spotting his own gun lying halfway up the slope, Livingston ran over and scooped it up. Then he lay flat behind a small boulder.

Several of the Germans opened fire, and Ogan dropped to his belly. They shot wide of Lambert; they obviously wanted him alive, to draw the others out.

The guns fell silent. Despite the crisp coursing of the

stream and the low idling of the truck, there was an eerie silence.

"Give yourselves up!" one of the Germans shouted. "There is nowhere you can go!"

Livingston looked back. Weyers had given up searching for his gun, was standing still, his chin resting in his hand; Colon continued to lean through the windshield, stiff as a statue. Suddenly, the South African began pitching pebbles at the cabin. Colon turned angrily.

Weyers put up a finger to his lips, then pointed from the gas tank of the truck to the road. He threw his hands apart, indicating an explosion.

Colon smiled and looked at Livingston, who nodded. Colon reached into his pocket and flipped a box of matches to Weyers, who had already opened the gas tank and stuffed a handkerchief in. Watching them, Livingston hoped—prayed—that they didn't hurt all the horses. The lieutenant motioned for Ogan to wait where he was, then dug his toes into the soft bank: He'd have to be ready to bolt the instant the truck was out of the gully.

Weyers signaled to Colon, who had moved behind the wheel. When the private gave him the okay, Weyers ignited the fabric and put his shoulder to the truck. When Colon hit the gas, Weyers gave the vehicle a hefty push.

Mud pelted him, but the South African kept shoving hard and suddenly the truck was free, shooting up the incline and onto the road. Inside, realizing that the enemy would have a shot at him if he left by one of the doors, Colon turned, squeezed through the rear windshield, and shot across the back of the truck; he jumped just as flame and shrapnel sprayed across the road.

The moment the truck blew up, Livingston ran ahead, followed by Ogan. The roar of the explosion drowned out the cries of the horses and men; it also did most of the dirty work. None of the Germans was moving, and many of the horses also had been killed.

Livingston looked across the field, breathed easier

when he saw that there were at least seven animals left.
Most had fled; by a stroke of luck, one was held back
by his dead rider. The man's boot was stuck in the stirrup
and the horse was running in a tight circle, trying un-
successfully to dislodge him. Ogan hurried over and
snatched the reins. Pulling the dead man free, he
mounted up and rode after the other horses. Livingston
checked on the Germans while Weyers tended to Lambert.

Colon joined the lieutenant. "What's the story, sir?"

"All but two of them are dead."

"Want me to put 'em on ice?"

Livingston shook his head. "I need you to give Ken a
hand."

Colon's eyes narrowed. "Are we going to *leave* them
alive—sir?"

"The horses are your only concern, Private."

"Sir, with all due respect, may I remind you that it's
quite possible these men will be found?"

"That's very likely. But what will they tell anyone?
That we got away? German command will realize that
anyway, when these men fail to report back. Now go
help Ogan with the horses, Colon. We're wasting time."

Saluting perfunctorily, Colon ran to the field while
Livingston took the IDs from the dead *unterwachtmeister*
and four other men. He blindfolded the two who survived, and lashed them to a dead horse. He then found
men whose uniforms would fit. Stripping the bodies, he
changed and brought clothes to Weyers and Lambert.
The Frenchman was sitting on the ground, rubbing the
back of his head and scanning the carnage with pain-
racked eyes.

"How is he, Wings?"

"Baffled, as usual."

Lambert looked back. "I won't even kick your balls
for that remark. Whatever happened here, I like what I
see, I'm alive to see it, and that's all that matters."

Weyers grinned. "Is it? Well, try these knickers on for size. We're going to have to make the rest of the journey on horseback."

Lambert's anguished eyes turned to Livingston. *"Vraiment?"*

The lieutenant nodded.

"With saddles?"

Livingston nodded again.

Lambert sighed. "Then it's not so bad. I'll be sore, but at least only the mount will be gelded."

After complimenting Weyers on his resourceful use of the truck, Livingston headed toward the stream, where one of the horses had doubled back and was drinking.

Livingston shook his head. If, in Uryupinsk, someone had told him that they'd be members of the German *kavallerie* before noon, he'd have told them they were crazy. But Force Five luck had held true, and for the second time in one day, nothing had gone as planned. He hoped that would change when they got to Stalingrad. If they did anything to the toxic gas but sink it straight to the bottom of the Volga, it would be the end of the city . . . and of Force Five.

Chapter Five

The horses were less efficient and far less comfortable than the truck.

In the truck, the men knew they'd get inside the relatively warm cabin every so often. Now there was nothing but a long day's travel into the bitter wind. When it came pounding off the plain, it was oppressive, causing the men to stop and turn sideways to avoid its full, frigid fury.

The horses also had to be rested and fed. No one in any of the villages protested when the soldiers commandeered meals for themselves and feed for the horses. However, all were downright amazed when, after they were brought to them, the German cavalrymen paid for them.

As they rode, Livingston was struck by the utter desolation of the countryside. Each village was more or less a self-contained society, only vaguely aware of towns up or down the road. Most of the people still got about on carts and horses, which explained the lack of good roads and the underdevelopment of the vast stretches of hills and plains between the towns. He mused that if the efforts being applied to the war had been turned to nurturing the Russian land and people, they'd be a most formidable nation.

By nightfall, as the weatherbeaten markers announcing Stalingrad dropped from triple to double digits, the villages became larger—and the German presence in most became pronounced. After a brush with a group of drunken soldiers outside of Anateka—Lambert sent them on their way with a pack of cigarettes—it became imperative to avoid the main road. However, the terrain proved so uneven that they had no choice but to abandon the horses and go the rest of the way on foot. They stripped off the saddles, weighted them with stones, cracked the ice of a small pond, and sunk them; they left the animals there as well. If the unbranded horses were discovered, it was unlikely they'd be traced to the missing unit.

It was well after eight o'clock when the men finally sat down beneath a rock ledge to get their bearings.

"That last village was Elistalovsky," Livingston said, consulting Mikhail's map. "That means we have to make our way around Stalingrad, get to the Volga, cross it, and hope that one of our contacts is still there."

"Ford the Volga without a boat." Lambert snickered. "We'd stand a better chance contacting General Paulus and offering to play poker for the city."

Weyers brayed, "With your luck, we'd lose the city *and* our shirts."

"Lieutenant," Colon said, "I'm concerned about what we do if the Russkies *ain't* waitin' for us."

"Then we just follow the river. Eventually, the German convoy will turn up."

"And what'll we use to sink it?"

"We'll have to find a way to get on board, punch a hole with explosives, or start a fire."

"What about Stalingrad?" Weyers asked. "We'll have to pass through German checkpoints."

Ogan answered, "The Russians usually try to sneak supplies into the city at night. We can probably pass as a patrol trying to keep them out."

"*Bien!*" Lambert said. "We get past the Jerries and get shot by the Reds."

"The Russians won't shoot," Ogan said. "The Germans are low on supplies as well. The Russians won't risk losing a fight and having their goods captured."

Weyers went off to urinate, muttering that no one ever lost his life by being prepared for a Russian, Czech, or Pole to do the *wrong* thing.

Deciding not to advance until after midnight, the men took advantage of their relative security to sleep. At 1 A.M., cold but rested, they moved through the fringes of the city.

The suburbs had fallen months before. The inhabitants had abandoned their burned-out homes, farms, and shops, and the Germans had pressed on to the city. Only when the men reached a bluff that overlooked Stalingrad itself did they pause.

This wasn't a city under siege. From all appearances, it was a dead city. The skeletons of modern buildings and factories stood beside the ruins of log huts, all of them shrouded in black smoke. Even at night, dark plumes could be seen churning up from the rubble, blotting out the cold clouds and full moon.

Weyers said, "You tellin' me there's people alive inside that?"

"Like ants," Ogan said. "The resistance . . . the life is all underground."

They started walking down. On the outskirts of the city, they passed the burned-out shell of a ten-story grain elevator. According to reports, that had been the scene of the area's fiercest fighting, the forty defenders having held out for ten days before being overwhelmed by sheer force of numbers. As they passed in silence, the edifice seemed to call out to them, the wind moaning, weeping, as it whipped through shattered windows and the huge holes in the walls.

The Germans held nine-tenths of the city. Those who saw the five men in cavalry jackets paid them no attention; no one wanted to go over and question them, lose his place around a campfire. Though it may have been a trick of the firelight, it seemed to Livingston that the soldiers he saw were unnaturally thin and haggard.

By 4 A.M., a day after landing on the farm, and a full day behind schedule, the men reached the high bluffs overlooking the Volga. The winds here were vicious and, from what they could see by searchlights on the German bank, the waters were less inviting still.

The river was approximately one hundred meters wide, with broken reeds, mud, and bomb craters lining either shore. The splintered pier where they were supposed to have met their Russian contacts was roughly two hundred meters upstream and apparently deserted.

"It's only an hour until sunrise," Livingston said. "We'd better move quickly if we want to cross while it's still dark."

From behind a shattered antiaircraft gun that had been destroyed in the Luftwaffe raids of August, Lambert and Ogan took turns scanning the pier for signs of one of the partisans. Weyers was sent back a few hundred meters, toward the city, to keep watch, while Livingston and Colon went north to try to find a boat, since the few bridges that spanned the river had been destroyed, and they'd freeze if they tried to swim across.

Just beyond a sharp bend in the river, with the sun rising on the opposite shore, the two men noticed several small wooden rowboats tied beneath a crumbling dock. Judging from the surroundings—a gazebo, benches, a maypole—the boats must have been used for summer holiday rowing on the river. Fortunately, they were only visible in the early morning when the sun slanted directly along the river; otherwise, they were hidden in the shadow of the dock.

Livingston and Colon hurried back to gather their companions.

"*Ah, bonjour,*" Lambert said, lowering his gun as they approached.

"See anything, Rotter?"

"*Non.* The reeds haven't moved, the water hasn't rippled, and the moonlight hasn't caught a puff of frozen breath."

"We'll go over anyway," Livingston said. "They may have decided to give us twenty-four hours before—"

The crunch of pebbles underfoot came from behind, and the men dropped and spun. Gazing back, they saw Weyers hurrying toward them. He was waving them on.

"Get the hell out, a bloody army's on the way!"

Livingston jumped up. "Are they after us?"

"Yes—but it's too long to explain. Just *move out!*"

The men ran along the bluff, then down the slope toward the riverbank. Breathless, they rushed to the dock and untied two of the wide rowboats; Weyers hopped into Lambert's boat, Ogan and Livingston rowing the second, with Colon watching their rear. The instant they started across, the boats were drawn downriver by the rapid current.

"Shit and damn!" the Frenchman bellowed, as the boats immediately turned their bows toward the south. "We'll go two meters down for every meter we go across!"

"Then row *harder!*" Weyers roared.

As he leaned into his oar, the boat began to pinwheel, scooting past the second boat, toward the bend—and the Germans beyond.

"*Slow down*, Weyers! My arms are too short to keep up!"

The South African slowed as the Germans came into

view. The boat stopped spinning but was still being drawn quickly downriver.

In the other boat, Livingston studied the Germans in the glow of the rising sun. They were watching over their Karabiners, waiting until he and his men were within range of the powerful rifles. The men might look gaunt, but the lieutenant had no doubt that their eyesight was fine. He'd never felt more like a sitting duck in his life.

When they were just over halfway across the river, Livingston heard the German *oberfeldwebel* give the order to fire. He was about to order the men to jump overboard and use the boats for cover, when he heard shots—not from Colon or from the Germans, but from the dock on the eastern side of the river.

The spray from the Degtyarev DP1928 light machine gun drove the enemy back. There was a commotion on the German side as soldiers shouldered their stolen Soviet-made PPsh submachine guns and fired at the ramshackle pier. Livingston yelled for his men to put their backs into the rowing before they got caught in the cross fire. Suddenly, the shooting on the Russian side stopped and someone bolted from a clump of reeds. With both hands, the newcomer grabbed the bow eye of Livingston's boat and waded backward, toward the shore. After the men had scurried up the rocky embankment, the young man motioned for them to continue running, then returned to the river and pulled the other boat to shore. A grateful Lambert jumped to safety and followed his comrades, barely pausing when he stumbled over the frozen body of a dead dog, one of five lying on the rocks.

When they were all atop the embankment, the young man reclaimed his Degtyarev and yelled, *"Edetyeh syudah!"* Leaping over the dogs, he led the men into a deep trench that had been dug in the field.

As they lay there, catching their breath in cold, painful gulps, Livingston studied their benefactor. He was very young, still a teenager, of medium height. Even though he wore several layers of clothing, the lieutenant could tell he was powerfully built. He moved with confidence and agility, and though he was soaked up to the waist, he seemed heedless of the cold. He wasn't shivering, nor did his expression show any discomfort. It was a stoic face, the cheekbones and nose Asiatic, with a stubble of beard. His eyes were brown but seemed even darker, set deep beneath heavy brows. He looked as hungry and tired as the Germans they'd seen, but there also seemed to be a touch of nobility about the man . . . in the way he carried his head, in the alertness of the eyes, in the clear disregard he had for his own safety or comfort.

When they had all recovered somewhat, the man pulled a sack from a niche hacked in the hard dirt wall. He withdrew a wheel of cheese and a canteen, offering them to the newcomers.

Livingston shook his head. "Thank you, *nyet.* Are you Vlasov?"

The Russian took a swig from the canteen. "*Da.* Andrei Vlasov. *Kutahnybody sidyesi gavoreet puh Ruskyeh?*"

Livingston looked at Ogan.

"He wants to know if any of us speaks Russian."

Livingston shook his head. "Just English, German, or French."

Andrei didn't seem pleased. He capped the canteen, then pointed across the river. "Leonid?"

Livingston shrugged, but Weyers said, "Bad news, chum, but the Nazis have your brother."

Livingston shot the corporal a look. "How do you know?"

"That's what I was yelling about before. While I was watching, the Jerries caught a Russian."

"Jerries?" Andrei said with alarm. "*Nyemetsky?*"

"*Da,*" Ogan said. "*Nyemetsky*—the Germans."

"He was coming from a tunnel when they grabbed

him," Weyers went on. "From what I gathered, they'd been looking for this tunnel which the Russians've been using to ferry supplies all the way from the goddamn cliffs into Stalingrad itself. When they saw this Leonid fellow, they followed him and found the tunnel. I gather there were still Russians inside, though, because he tried to stall the Jerries. He told them there were partisans on the river, waiting for him."

"But he couldn't have known that!" Livingston said.

"That's just it. He lied, not knowing we were there. The Germans took him away, then came to check, which is when I took off."

"Where's Leonid now?" Ogan asked.

"I have no idea."

Livingston regarded Andrei. "Where is Masha?"

Pulling a foot-long dagger from a sheath he wore at his waist, the now distraught young man scratched a diagram in the earth. "Stalingrad," he said, pointing to a mark. "Volga." He traced the course of the river. Then he drew four ovals. *"Yat,"* he said.

Ogan consulted his phrase book. "The poison . . . the boats with the poison."

"Da—boats," Andrei said, then crossed out two of the ovals. As the men watched, puzzled, he drew a second line, which roughly paralleled the course of the river and ended in Stalingrad. *"Poeezd,"* he said. "Masha."

Ogan sat back. *"Poeezd?"*

Andrei nodded heavily.

"What is it?" Livingston demanded.

"Christ Jesus," he said. "What he said is that the shipment has been split up—that two of the gas tanks are no longer with the convoy."

"Where the hell are they?"

"On a train," Ogan said gravely, "bound for the heart of the city."

"A two-pronged attack."

"So it would seem."

Pointing at the tracks he'd drawn, Andrei said, "Masha."

"She's gone ahead to reconnoiter," Livingston said.

Breathing deeply, in a clear effort to control his emotions, Andrei pointed toward the city and said, *"Kak mazhna skayeya. Zavod!"*

"He's saying something about a meeting," Ogan said, "a factory." He flipped through the pages, then said haltingly, *"Yah . . . upzhdal na payezd . . . samalyawt?"*

"Da! Da!"

"That's what it is," Ogan said. "We're supposed to rendezvous with Masha at a factory."

There was a lengthy silence, after which Lambert said, "A train. How the hell are we going to dump a trainload of gas?"

"Assuming we can even get close to it," Weyers said. "It's probably an armored train, and protected up the bum."

Andrei poked Weyers. "Leonid," he said, then sketched out a circle. "Stalingrad." He handed the knife to the South African, urged him to make a mark in the circle.

Weyers shook his head. "I don't know where they took him. *Nyet!*"

Andrei looked imploringly at Ogan. The Englishman managed to explain, after which the partisan snatched the knife and, in a fit of fury, drove it over and over into the side of the trench. The other men watched in silence until, his anger spent, the Russian slumped down.

"Remind me never to piss him off," Lambert said with a stiff smile.

After a moment, Livingston motioned for the men to

gather in a tight circle. Andrei remained where he was, his knees drawn up, face between them.

"Obviously, we're going to have to split up," the lieutenant said. "Each group will have less firepower, but at least it will be easier to come and go without being seen."

"The thing is," Ogan said, "if either group fails, the entire mission fails. The Germans will still have enough gas to cover the Russian strongholds."

"Unfortunately, there isn't enough time to hop from one site to the other."

"No argument. I'm just saying there's no room at all for error."

Weyers was looking at the Russian. "Y'know, I'll bet this bloke's been here since yesterday, still as a broken watch, waiting for us while his brother made supply runs into the city." The South African faced Livingston. "We owe him. We can't just leave Leonid to die."

Ogan said, "I sympathize, Corporal, but where do you expect to get the manpower?"

"All I need is one man. Me."

"No," Livingston said, "no one goes anywhere alone. But I like the idea for another reason. We'll divide into three groups. Ken—you and Andrei will try to get to Masha and the train. Weyers and Lambert, you two will meet the convoy. Colon and I will go in and try to find Leonid, then wait here. If one or the other of the shipments gets through, we can be a stopgap."

"I like it," Weyers said, and when no one had any objections, Ogan went over and explained the plan to Andrei. At first, the Russian protested, insisting that he wanted to rescue his own "*brat*." But Ogan convinced him that Livingston and Colon were well suited for the task, and besides, he needed the Russian to help him get to the train.

Andrei didn't seem to hear the last part. He was

busy staring at Colon. *"Italianski-Americanski?"* he asked.

Colon stared back. "Something wrong?"

The others watched tensely as Andrei reached into his pocket; he withdrew a watch and opened the lid, showed Colon a photograph. *"Atyets."*

"His father," Ogan explained, looking at the picture. He asked Andrei, "And who is the other gentleman?"

"Italianski-Americanski. Houdini."

Lambert said, "The guy wasn't Italian—his name was Weiss."

"When in Russia," Ogan said, "people become what the government favors. Houdini obviously toured here, and Andrei's father must have met him."

"Terrific," Colon said. "We're facing death, and I gotta listen to some guy's life story."

"I *believe,* Private, he's trying to pay you a compliment. Obviously, Houdini meant something to Andrei's father, and to Andrei."

"Oh. Like a hero, you mean."

"Possibly."

Colon's expression softened. "Well, in that case—great. Thank him. Tell him we're gonna do an escape trick that'll put Harry to shame."

Ogan translated as best he could, and the Russian eased visibly.

The town of Novocherkassk, where Andrei said the transfer had taken place, was just two hundred kilometers away. Both the train and the convoy would reach Stalingrad as early as that evening.

That left just over half a day to intercept them. And to capture the train, which was the only way they'd get the gas far enough from the city. They couldn't even worry about keeping it out of Russian hands. Keeping it out of Russian lungs, off Russian flesh, was a more pressing matter.

After consulting maps that were stored in an iron box in the trench, the three teams set out. As they stood on the field, well beyond the range of the German guns, Andrei embraced each of the men. And each man, including Colon, returned the gesture, warmly.

Chapter Six

Through Ogan, Andrei told Livingston and Colon to wait until six-thirty before going across. That was when the night guard was relieved on the western bank; there was always a gap of two or three minutes while the newcomers were briefed and settled in for the eight-hour shift.

The two would be crossing much higher on the river than they had earlier. Andrei gave them a rubber raft that was kept in the trench for their regular passages; it bore the name *Nevsky*, one of the Russian gunboats that had patroled the river before the German bombers destroyed them all.

Andrei had also given them a password: *"Sorahk."*

Forty.

The number of men and women who died defending the grain elevator. Since they were dressed in German uniforms, if they had to deal with any Russians in the city, it was the only word that would help them.

Ogan, Andrei, Lambert, and Weyers all set out to the east, turning south once they were behind the guns and out of the view of the Germans. At 6:15, Livingston and Colon headed for the river. With field glasses provided by Andrei, Livingston studied the cliffs. When the watch was changed, they rushed into the river.

This crossing was utterly uneventful. A year before, the Germans would never have been so sloppy as to leave such a gap in their guard. But the prospect of spending another winter in Russia had obviously taken its toll on morale. Escott had told him that 200,000 Germans had already died here, and that Stalingrad had been referred to, in one German communiqué, as the "mass grave of the Wehrmacht." Livingston suspected that the only reason they pursued the Russians so doggedly, still, was because they knew that victory was their only ticket home.

The men paddled across quickly, hid the raft beneath the pier in the holiday area, then hiked up the bluff.

They'd decided that the best tack would be to go to the tunnel. There would still be soldiers about, and with any luck, Livingston could use his adopted rank of *unterwachtmeister* to find out where Leonid had been taken.

Reaching the top of the cliff, they walked to where Weyers had been stationed. As they neared the foot of the dirt road, they saw at least thirty soldiers gathered around a hole. There was a tree stump lying behind it, a false top to the entrance of the tunnel.

As they descended, the lieutenant noticed a severe-looking *hauptfeldwebel* standing beside an aide. The regimental sergeant major was thumping the side of his boot with a dry tree branch, watching the proceedings from behind thick glasses. As a senior NCO, he outranked Livingston, who was posing as a junior NCO. So much for walking over and demanding the information.

Thinking quickly, Livingston stepped up to the NCO and stood at attention.

"Reporting as ordered!"

The sergeant major peered through the fat lenses. "As ordered?"

"Yes, *Hauptfeldwebel*. By *Rittmeister* Krebs."

The *hauptfeldwebel* tapped his cleft chin. "I have never heard of him."

"We are just up from the Caucuses, *Hauptfeldwebel*. We heard that volunteers were needed to enter the tunnel and flush out the enemy."

"And has the cavalry nothing better to do than back up my infantry?"

"*Nein, Hauptfeldwebel*. The *rittmeister* simply thought that if the infantry were needed in the city, we might be able to relieve them here." He moved closer, said knowingly, "Our unit doesn't go into action until the ships from the Fatherland arrive. He thought it might be useful to get this business over with quickly."

"I see." The slender man studied Livingston a moment longer, then pointed the branch toward the tunnel. "We already have volunteers inside. And we have men on the other end, inside an abandoned factory." He smiled mirthlessly. "I give those Russian *hunds* credit for having dug and operated this tunnel without our knowledge for nearly a year. However, the end is near."

"Are you certain the enemy won't take their own lives?"

The noncom eyed Livingston suspiciously. "You have not seen much action, have you, *Unterwachtmeister*?"

"Yes, *Hauptfeldwebel*—a good deal, in fact."

"Then how is it you do not know the Russian mind?"

Livingston frowned; mercifully, the NCO did not wait for an answer.

"As long as the Russians believe they can kill one of our men, they will not take their own lives. Only when we smoke them out with tear gas do they shoot themselves. At the moment, we are trying a new approach. We are rounding up several of the men and women we've captured. When they're here, we'll begin shooting them until the men inside surrender."

Livingston didn't have to look to know that Colon had tensed behind him. He didn't blame him, but the last time the private had torn loose, in Algiers—when they were trying to steal a motorcycle—they'd been lucky to get away with their lives. Livingston looked back at the tunnel. As he turned, he fired a cautioning glance at Colon, whose eyes were angry slits.

"Let me go in there, *Hauptfeldwebel*," Livingston said. "I think I can bring them out."

"How will you do that?"

"Earlier, we overheard some partisans use a password by the river. I can use that to lure them out."

"What was the password?"

"*Pavadze*," he said, "a nickname they have for Stalin. I can fire several shots, give the Russians the password, and convince them that our soldiers are dead and they should come out. That way, you will have them *and* the prisoners you've already—"

Livingston's words were cut off as a big, noisy Opel Blitz truck arrived with the prisoners. There were eight men and six women, all tied one to the other by their hands, so they couldn't run. Livingston had no idea whether Leonid was among them.

"*Hauptfeldwebel*," he said urgently, "will you let me try?"

"I commend your courage, but I think not. We can't spare the rations to keep prisoners anyway."

"And what of the Russians in the tunnel?"

"They'll die too, of course."

"What I mean is, the tunnel probably hasn't a single support. How long before one of the enemy realizes that all he needs to do is start shooting to bring the ceiling down? How many of *our* men will survive such a cave-in?"

The noncom eyed Livingston. "It's possible." He cupped a hand to his mouth. "Hans! Tell the men in the tunnel to withdraw! I'll be sending one of them back in with a message to relay to the *wurm-stichig* Russians."

Livingston was caught off guard. "*Hauptfeldwebel*, please, allow *me* to serve the Fatherland—"

"No. You're quite right about the tunnel, *Unterwachtmeister*, and I thank you for your help. But these men have earned the right to finish the job they started."

Livingston looked at Colon. There was no choice, now, but to fight for the lives of the Russian prisoners. Livingston unbuttoned his holster as he backed toward where the private was standing. His plan was to kill the men nearest him, then get to the truck and arm the Russians. But as Livingston approached, he heard footsteps behind him; he turned and saw Colon walking swiftly toward the tunnel.

It was too late to stop him and, swearing under his breath, Livingston had no choice but to wait and see what the private was going to do.

Lambert's thighs still ached from the horse, and now his feet hurt from traipsing across the hard ground. Worse, because he was walking briskly to keep up with Weyers, his chest and sides stung with every frigid breath. And to cap off the morning, as the pair passed through a village, the slate gray skies opened and began dumping snow. The temperature plunged.

"Do you think we should steal a horse and cart?" Lambert asked through his chattering teeth.

The South African shook his head. "We need to be mobile. Besides, in this weather, a cart and a horse . . ."

He didn't bother to finish the sentence. He just sneered up at the sky and shook his big head.

Lambert knew what Weyers meant. They'd get bogged down within minutes, or else the horse would freeze to death. There was no choice but to walk, and the only thing that kept him going was rage: anger that the Germans in the convoy were probably warm and comfortable in their death-boats.

The morning dragged as the snow fell without respite.

Visibility was less than a few meters; when the winds kicked in, the cold drew tears from their eyes, and their vision was blurred even further. Both men were forced to walk with their faces averted, to protect them from the battering winds.

They proceeded blindly. It wasn't until Lambert slipped on a patch of ice that they realized they were on a lake. As Weyers helped him up, the Frenchman happened to look to the side, then screamed for his companion to turn around.

Nearly flat on its back now, the snow-covered B-17 looked like a white dragon, its tail fin the head, its fuselage the long neck, its wings two immense legs. The men slogged toward the plane, Lambert slipping several times as the winds howled across the open expanse and literally knocked him down.

Reaching the aircraft, the men crawled up the fuselage and entered the hatch. They stepped down gingerly because lake water had frozen along the length of the plane's interior, making it extremely slippery.

Though it was still well below zero, being out of the wind caused Lambert to shudder with relief. He pulled the stiff scarf from his face, then began stamping the ice from his boots and trousers. He peered down the darkened fuselage.

"*Alors*, you're the aviation expert. Could they have walked away from this?"

"Quite possibly. There was no fire, and very little damage to the fuselage. Captain Kane did a hell of a job bringing her in. There's a man I want to buy a dinner."

"The question is, why didn't we see them? They were supposed to make for the pier."

"Maybe they took shelter in the village. Not everyone is stupid enough to travel during a blizzard."

The airplane creaked and bent slightly; a hairline crack appeared in the ice beneath them. Lambert looked out a window.

"True," the Frenchman said, "but I wonder." He walked ahead, into the upside-down cockpit, and lit a match. "*Regardez!* The maps are missing."

Weyers glanced toward where the navigator had been sitting. "Maybe he took them. Or they coulda sunk."

"*C'est possible.* Yet—if they were stolen, it would explain how we were found out in Uryupinsk. It may also be the reason the Germans split the shipment of gas. Perhaps they figured out what we were up to."

Weyers's massive shoulders dropped. "If that's the case, then they'll be expecting us on the river."

"At the very least."

"What do you mean?"

"I mean, if they've found the cavalry unit we took on—which by now they surely have—they'll also know how we're dressed."

"We won't even get *near* the boats."

Lambert stamped his feet to stay warm. "*Alors*, we're not going to give up. We'll just have to figure out a way around it."

Weyers sat heavily on the ice. "Sure. Maybe the Japanese have the right idea after all. You go in not planning to come out. Makes things a lot easier."

"Not Le Rodeur," Lambert said. "He plans to come out, and does. Never failed yet."

Warming, Lambert reached up and felt around in the nook behind the cylindrical panel light.

"What're you looking for?"

"Abel's cigarettes, but they're gone. The Huns were here all right."

"How do you know? Maybe Abel took them."

"*Non.* He told me that he only smoked when he flew." Raising his fists, Lambert cried, "I promise, *mes comarades*, the enemy will regret ever having set *eyes* on this aircraft . . . or on me."

"You have a plan?"

"A plan? I don't *need* a plan, Wings, I am Le Rodeur. I *always* find a way."

Weyers had unholstered his gun to check it over; he scowled. "I hope so, Rotter, because it's beginning to look like your wits and my fists are all we've got left. Take a look."

Weyers handed Lambert the pistol, and he examined it: The chamber had cracked, a combination of the cold and shoddy manufacture. He quickly checked his own weapon, which was intact, and exhaled loudly.

Weyers grinned. "Confidence isn't as good as a working Luger, is it?"

Lambert said nothing as he holstered the gun. He didn't have to. The sigh had said it all.

An hour after setting out, Ogan and Andrei reached a point nearly six kilometers north of the city, where the Volga narrowed sufficiently so that a person could wade across. It wasn't what Ogan wanted to do, but there was no alternative. As Andrei reminded him, they had to cross sooner or later. And it was better now, under cover of the sudden snow squall, than later. At least this way, they wouldn't be seen by anyone on the other side.

Andrei removed his coat, shoes, and socks, and instructed Ogan to do likewise. With a few words and gestures, the Russian indicated that, unlike before, when he had gone in only up to his waist, the river here would be well over that. Their coats would absorb the water and freeze when they came ashore, weighing them down, and making it impossible to move.

Reluctantly, the Englishman followed Andrei's lead, then waded in quickly.

How the Russians did it, regularly, was beyond the Englishman's comprehension. How they avoided frostbite and gangrene—how *anyone* did—was also a mystery. He had heard of Tibetans whose feet were so tough they

could walk barefoot across sharp rocks and ice; perhaps
the Russians had a similar resistance to cold.

Ogan, like the Germans, did not.

The water bit like thousands of tiny needles. He felt
the burning chill on his legs, feet, and waist; nearly as
bad were the wind and snow that lashed his upper torso
and face. The wet snow also collected quickly on his
coat, which he held over his head, causing it to double
in weight. Ogan was glad, at least, for the current that
pushed and threatened to knock them down; it gave them
something other than pain to concentrate on as they
crossed.

When they came ashore, his chest was numb, his legs
were on fire, and his head throbbed viciously from the
cold. He pulled on his coat and rubbed his arms hard as
they walked, well understanding just why the Germans
were bringing poison gas to Stalingrad rather than digging in for another winter.

They followed the river north, until the snow became
blinding. Afraid of falling into the deep-drifting snow,
they took shelter in an abandoned German tank; they left
the hatch open, lest it freeze shut, and kept out the
weather by stuffing the Russian's coat in the cupola.

Ogan was glad to be out of the storm, and assuaged
his guilt by telling himself that the train would also be
forced to stop. Andrei muttered that he hoped his sister
and brother were all right, then went ferreting about the
tank for stores. He found neither food nor drink, but
there was a working radio, and Ogan flicked it on. Despite the storm, they were able to pick up a broadcast
from Germany, a speech Hitler had made the night before, at a dinner party.

The Führer was saying, "There stands a certain town
that bears the name of Stalin himself. I wanted to take
the place, and, you know, we've done it. We've got it,
really, except for a few enemy positions still holding out.
Now people say, 'Why don't they finish the job more

quickly?' Well, I prefer to do the job with quite small assault groups. Time is of no consequence at all.''

Andrei recognized the voice, and asked Ogan what Hitler was saying. Using his book, Ogan translated the gist of the speech. When he was finished, the Russian spat, then shut his eyes and went to sleep.

Chapter Seven

There were four soldiers at the entrance to the tunnel, and Livingston watched as Colon walked over to them. The private didn't speak much German, but that didn't matter: Colon was not a man who relied on words to make a point.

The four soldiers paid him little attention as he approached. As Colon neared the group, Livingston looked about, trying to decide where to make his own stand.

He decided on the truck. There were just three Germans, and if Colon did what he anticipated, they would give him little trouble. Turning, he walked over, all the while watching Colon from the corner of his eye.

When the private reached the tunnel, he said something to a soldier who was smoking; Livingston assumed that he asked the man for a cigarette, for the man reached into his coat pocket. He also bought himself an extra heartbeat of life: Colon knew where *his* hands were, so he shot the other two before gunning down the smoker. He was in the tunnel and gone before anyone else realized who had fired or where.

At the first report, Livingston drew and shot the sergeant major through the forehead. Then he stepped up to the cab and killed the driver and another soldier. He

spun. There were just three other men, standing with
shovels and picks midway between the truck and the dirt
road. The lieutenant shot two of them before his gun
jammed; tossing it aside, he ran at the third man.

The soldier had a pick and, to Livingston's surprise,
he threw it like an Olympic hammer. The head hit Livingston's chest and knocked him down; the next thing he
knew, the soldier had dropped onto his chest with one
knee, and was flailing at his face.

Though the German was at least ten years younger and
twenty pounds heavier, his blows were stiff, their impact
muted by the gloves and layers of clothing he was wearing. Livingston bucked and tried to roll over, but the
German straddled him and pressed his forearm across the
American's neck, cutting off his air.

Livingston wasn't able to pull off his own gloves, and
the blows he threw were dull and ineffective. He cast
desperately around for something to use as a weapon,
and spotting a rock, he was unable to wrench it from the
frozen soil. Then he saw the dagger hanging from the
belt of the soldier's quilted over-trousers. Overcome with
rage, wanting to lash out with his fists, the German had
neglected it. It was an oversight that would cost him his
life. Grabbing the hilt, Livingston pushed the blade up,
through the man's chin.

Blood poured onto Livingston's hands and coat as the
German sat up. Stunned, the soldier rose unsteadily and
felt the knife handle with disbelief. Then his eyes rolled
back into his head and he twisted, falling across Livingston. The American pushed him aside, then looked down.

The bastard wasn't dead. He was staring up, wheez-
ing, pawing at his chin, trying to dislodge the knife. The
blood in the wound bubbled with every breath.

Livingston reached down and pulled out the blade.
There was no time to do anything for the man. Throwing
the dagger to the Russian prisoner so they could free

themselves, Livingston took a P.38 from a dead soldier, shot the wounded man, and ran to the tunnel.

Colon liked tight places.

As a child in Pittsburgh, he'd loved storm drains. Crawl spaces. Closets. Hiding under beds. There was something dangerous and exciting about a hole or a close space—no room for error. Here, neither he nor the enemy could turn and run. They had to fight it out.

He moved through the pitch-black tunnel by wriggling along on his forearms. Progress was slow, not only because of the way he was traveling, but also due to the tunnel itself. While building it, the Russians had encountered roots and rocks that they hadn't bothered to dislodge. They slowed his progress. They had also encountered two building foundations, which they simply went around. There was no way to see these changes coming; one first had to run into them. Fortunately, the floor itself was relatively smooth, worn flat by countless people having wormed their way through with crates and sacks. He felt a welling of pride for the Russians when he considered that supplies could only be pushed through the tunnel. Each passage had to take at least an hour in the dark—something that would have given even nonclaustrophobics pause.

When he heard German voices coming from up ahead, Colon stopped and listened, trying to figure out how far away they were. But it was impossible to gauge because sounds reverberated through the tunnel. However, as he crept along, he continued listening, for it occurred to him that other tunnels might connect with this one, and there was no time for a wrong turn. Though it caused his neck to cramp, he kept his head erect, face forward, to make certain he didn't miss the glow of any lights the Germans might be using.

Because he hadn't heard any German voices behind him after the shooting, he assumed Livingston had managed to take the others by surprise. He admired the Lieutenant enormously.but wished Livingston would save his attempts at persuasion and reasoning for when he had kids. Germans were for shooting on sight.

A glint of yellow light caught Colon's eye, and he stopped and listened. The Germans up ahead were whispering—from the few words he could make out, they were wondering why they hadn't heard anything else from the men outside.

Colon grinned wickedly. He enjoyed surprises. Unsheathing his dagger, he crawled ahead slowly.

As he entered the last long stretch of tunnel, one of the soldiers heard him. It was the soldier farthest from him; the German craned around slightly and shined the light around his comrades.

"Loben wir Gott!" the German said with relief.

Praise God your ass, Colon thought as he shielded his eyes with his free hand. *"Das licht!"* he complained, not even certain he'd said the right word. He must have; the other soldier apologized and turned the flashlight away, then began asking questions.

Colon didn't understand what the soldier was saying, nor did he care. As soon as he was beside the nearest of the men, he brought his right arm up along his side and plunged the knife through the man's open coat, into his heart. Squeezing past him before the others could react, he cut the next man's throat with a backward slash. Dousing the light, the last man crawled ahead.

Certain the German would be desperate enough to use his gun, Colon backed up and lay low, behind the two dead men. He pushed his fingers into his ears moments before a shot reverberated through the tunnel; it was followed by a scream as the sound shattered the soldier's eardrums. Colon waited several seconds. The ground was frozen sufficiently so that only a thin layer of dirt was dislodged by the shot. When the echoes died, Colon felt around for the flashlight. Switching it on, he pressed on through the dirt that hung suspended in the beam.

Less than three meters ahead, the German soldier was lying on his back, his arms across his face, his head rolling slowly from side to side. Colon put him from his misery by sliding the knife between his ribs, then snaked around the dead man. When he heard movement up ahead, he stopped and yelled along the tunnel.

"Sorahk!"

There was a heavy silence. After a few moments, he said, "Goddammit, yer pal *Andrei* sent me!"

There was more movement ahead, coming in his direction. Placing the flashlight on the ground, facing him, he lay on his belly with his palms turned toward the beams. The sound stopped and, suddenly, the flashlight seemed to float into the air. The beam played over and around him, settling briefly on the dead man.

"Shtah vi khatityeh?"

"I don't understand yer lingo. I only speak English . . . American."

"Amerikanski?"

"Yeah. Amerikansi. I killski Nazis." Colon pointed behind him. *"Nyet* Nazis. Coast clear."

The light was turned then, and illuminated the Russian. The wan, grizzled face nodded once, then motioned with its chin for Colon to follow.

"Nyet," Colon said, "they're waitin' for ya at that end. *Nazis."*

He pointed behind them. The Russian understood, and indicated for Colon to go back the way he'd come.

That was easier suggested than done. Colon quickly discovered that as difficult as it had been to move forward, it was much more difficult going backward. It was impossible to turn, and in order to move, he was forced to push with his hands and flop back, like a fish out of water. His arms quickly cramped, but there was no other way to negotiate the tunnel.

A half hour later he emerged with the two Russians in a raging snowstorm. Much to his surprise, Livingston was nowhere to be seen. After checking the dead Germans to make sure that none of the snow-covered forms was the lieutenant, he looked from the river to the city. Knowing the lieutenant and why they'd come, he turned and ran toward the city.

When the B-17 shuddered and sloped backward at an angle, Lambert and Weyers decided it was time to go.

The South African hurriedly finished etching the names of the B-17 crew members in the ice, then joined Lambert at the hatch on the top of the aircraft.

It was nearly ten. They'd been there an hour, and the storm had abated somewhat. They surveyed the layer of snow that covered the lake. The drooping plane had caused a weblike pattern of cracks that reached nearly to the shore; they had no idea how badly the ice itself may have split.

"What do you think?" Lambert asked.

"Does it matter? We've got to go."

Lambert went first, sliding down the fuselage and then holding out his arms for balance. When the ice held, Weyers joined him, and they began their slow, cautious trek toward the shore. Only a few slabs of ice had broken off from the rest and, although several spots were unsteady, they crossed the lake with no problem.

As they were about to enter the woods, Lambert suddenly stopped.

"What's wrong?"

The Frenchman eyed a high pile of snow for several seconds more, then went over and started brushing it off.

"It's a pile of rocks," Weyers grunted.

"*Non,*" Lambert said. "It's a grave."

"Impossible. The Germans ship their dead home, and the Russians bring them to their families. Anyway, it's too large for a grave."

Lambert was unconvinced, and began removing the topmost stones. A sick feeling welled in his gut, and he began pulling the rocks away more quickly. As he did so, he began to pant—not from exertion, but from anger.

"Say, mate, what the bloody hell is *wrong* with you?"

Lambert didn't answer. He pushed over a large slab, then stood back. His entire body trembled with fury as he stared down. Stared at the corpses of the pilot and copilot.

There was crystallized blood on their white flesh, and their feet and hands were bare. Someone had taken their shoes and gloves.

Weyers gazed openmouthed at the bodies. "The Jerry scum. They . . . *executed* them!"

Lambert regarded the men for a long moment. Then, slowly, he began to cover the grave. Weyers helped him.

They were nearly finished before Lambert spoke. "Whoever killed them may still be in the vicinity."

"Probably a patrol—a small outpost guarding this section of the river. The Jerries haven't that many men to spare this far from the city."

"However many there are, they'll be made to answer for what they've done."

Weyers regarded Lambert through the fast-fading storm. "Are you sure that's the right thing, Rotter? Risking our lives when we should be concentrating on that shipment?"

Lambert stood back and stared at the grave. "I'm sure."

The South African turned. Through the trees, he could just see the snowy slopes that led to the bluffs overlooking the Volga. "Well, the convoy'll be coming this way eventually. I suppose it doesn't matter where we meet it."

Uncharacteristically silent, Lambert made a cross from fallen branches and jammed it into the stones. Then he led the way southwest, to the cliffs. When they reached the top, they stopped to study the riverbank. There, Lambert saw what he'd hoped to find.

Smoke, rising from roughly a half kilometer downriver.

A bunker.

His eyes narrow, mouth uncharacteristically mean, Lambert moved quickly across the snow-covered expanse toward the German position.

After Ogan and Andrei had warmed slightly, he asked Andrei why it was necessary to go north to intercept a train that was coming from the south. Switching on a small, battery-powered instrument light, the Russian found a pencil and pad and began sketching a map of the trains.

Although the tracks paralleled the river in the south, they went wide around the city and came in from the north. Andrei explained that a quarter century before, when the system was built, it was the only way the line could be constructed without disturbing the city. Moreover, fishermen who plied the waters near the city had complained that, if the tracks ran by the river, the noise of the trains would frighten away the fish. The circuitous route also allowed farms in the north to use the trains to ship crops into the city—though few did because of the expense.

The German train would have to travel southward for approximately four kilometers before entering the terminal—a straight run through largely open fields. Somewhere along that stretch was where they'd have to attack. Asked what made him certain the Germans would not unload the gas before that, Andrei replied that only the terminal yard had the cranes and other equipment they'd need.

When the storm let up, the men pushed the stiffened coat from the opening. They had to struggle to dislodge it, working their hands around the sides, smacking off the snow, and finally pulling it in. Andrei bent and cracked the garment, then forced his arms through the frozen sleeves.

Suddenly, his head cocked like that of a wary deer. He pressed a finger to his lips and sat stone-still. Ogan listened.

Now the Englishman heard them too. Voices. German voices. Most likely a patrol that had also been waiting out the storm.

Andrei snapped off the light and buried his face in his coat, motioning for Ogan to do likewise. The Englishman understood. Rising from the turret, their frosty breath might well be spotted by the Germans.

The voices grew louder.

"—was Gerhardt's tank. The cannon was sabotaged, so they just left it."

The soldiers fell silent; Ogan could hear their heavy breathing, the crunch of boots on the fresh snow.

Then the crunching stopped.

"Look, there, at the canopy," someone said.

"Marks," said another. "They look like scratches."

"Animals that took shelter perhaps? Squirrels?"

"If so, we have dinner."

The coat! Ogan thought. *It had disturbed the snow!*

The crunching and the voices came closer. "Wouldn't it be nice if it were a pheasant seeking shelter?"

"With our luck, it will be a *peasant* who took shelter."

"*Wahrscheinlich!* I wonder how they taste!"

Andrei nudged Ogan, handed the Englishman his pistol. He motioned for him to put the gun to his chest. Ogan shook his head violently. There wasn't any way he'd kill the Russian.

Andrei also shook his head. Then he raised his hands, and Ogan understood: Andrei would pretend to be his prisoner.

Reluctantly, Ogan agreed and, turning his face toward the opening, yelled, *"Achtung! Mein kamerad!"*

He heard the distinctive sound of rifle bolts sliding into place. "Who's in there?"

"Trompeterreiter Wilhelm Keitel. I have a Russian prisoner with me. We came in to wait out the storm!"

Ogan heard several sets of feet headed toward the tank. Two ruddy faces peered in and seemed satisfied with what they saw; they pulled Andrei out, then helped Ogan from the tank.

Ogan stood on stiff legs as the squad *oberwachtmeister* came over. The gaunt NCO wore a sparse beard and an unfriendly expression.

"Well," he said, "a hero and his captive. Explain yourself, *Trompeterreiter.*"

Thinking quickly, Ogan said that his own company had been ambushed several kilometers to the north, and that he was the only survivor. He said he had managed to capture one of the Russians, and was bringing him in for questioning. The *oberwachtmeister* examined Ogan's papers, then looked the Englishman over.

"A hero," he said, "and a well-fed one at that. What did you have to eat, *Trompeterreiter?*"

"Sir, we killed and ate our horses. There was nothing to feed them, and they would have died anyway. We simply ceased being a cavalry unit and became infantry."

For a long moment, the NCO's face revealed nothing of what he was thinking. Then, suddenly, he broke into a broad smile.

"Very resourceful, Keitel. You will come with us, then, and will remain infantry. Ritzenthaler, Eichermann—take the prisoner."

Ogan watched as Andrei was pulled from the tank and pushed ahead. He resisted the urge to gun the men down. There were ten of them, plus the squad leader. Even if Andrei had a gun, it would be difficult to come out on top.

The squad marched through the snow, Ogan convivially sharing stories with the men as Andrei was repeatedly shoved into the snow and kicked by the soldiers who held him at riflepoint. For once, Ogan found himself wishing that Private Colon was there, and offered up a silent prayer.

As they passed the holiday area by the river, and turned to go up the dirt road that led to the city, Ogan's eyes suddenly went wide.

If there was a God, he thought, He had a curious flair for the dramatic. . . .

Chapter Eight

Upon reaching the mouth of the tunnel, Livingston heard a gunshot from deep inside. If it had dislodged any of the tunnel roof, Colon's retreat might be blocked, leaving them no choice but to continue ahead—right into the arms of the soldiers waiting at the opposite end. Rounding up a man and three of the fittest women from among the Russian prisoners, he communicated to them that he was going to the other side of the tunnel, and could use their help. They agreed without hesitation and, taking guns from the dead soldiers, the four Russians led the way.

The trip to the factory was uneventful, though Livingston noticed two packs of emaciated dogs running through the snow toward the river. He remembered the dead animals he'd seen on the other side, and presumed the dogs deserted the city whenever they ran out of food. If the animals found Stalingrad uninhabitable, he couldn't imagine how the Russians survived.

The group entered a wide, deserted square dominated by a larger-than-life-size statue of six children dancing in a circle. It was an incongruous sight amid all the carnage—charred wood jutting through the snow, bricks, and crumbled walls of buildings scattered around the square, twisted pipes and broken wire lying about. And yet, Livingston told himself, the statue was probably a sight that gave the defenders hope. Russian children had played here once before; they would play here again.

After crossing the square, Livingston followed the Russians down a broad avenue toward a towering gray tractor factory. As they neared, they slowed and walked quietly toward an open door. Livingston drew his pistol and entered.

He was inside a small room, a machine shop. Two young soldiers were squatting beside a lathe which, apparently, had been used to conceal the opening. Livingston approached and they looked up. When he was just a few steps away, he ordered them to raise their hands.

"What have we done, *Rittmeister*?"

"Just do as you're told," Livingston said, then summoned the Russians. The soldiers stared in stunned silence until the lieutenant had them bound to the lathe with electrical cord. One of them started shouting obscenities, calling Livingston a traitor, and was gagged; the other soldier looked frightened and said nothing.

Livingston bent over him.

"Early this morning, a man was captured at the other end of the tunnel, a young Russian named Leonid. Where is he?"

The youth swallowed hard. "They said they were going to question him and then take him to the gallery."

"Which gallery?"

"O–our *gallery*. Where things are . . . *shown* for the public."

Livingston felt a jolt. It couldn't be. It just couldn't be. He jammed his pistol in the holster; if he hadn't, he'd have used it.

"Where is this place?"

"It's—it's on the north side of the square."

Rushing outside, Livingston ran back toward the square. It probably hadn't been wise to leave the soldiers in the hands of the Russians, but at the moment that wasn't nearly as important as getting to Leonid before it was too late.

Passing the statue of the children, he turned down a small street on the northern side. He stopped short and stared at a sight he would never forget.

Seventeen men and six women hung naked from streetlights up and down both sides of the road. Around each of their necks was a cardboard sign that read, in both Russian and German, "We are partisans. We tried to kill German soldiers."

For several minutes, Livingston couldn't move. He gazed through the snow at the sadistic spectacle. The heels of several of the victims had been gnawed, probably by dogs leaping and nipping at them. But very little snow collected on them, meaning they were still warm enough to melt it.

The Germans must do this every day. Rise, eat, and execute prisoners.

His chest tight, Livingston walked along the street, looking up at each of the corpses. He felt neither the snow nor the wind, just the bile burning in his throat.

Yes, he thought, supplies were low. It was impractical to keep prisoners, other than the women who were kept for the soldiers, or the people who were used as bait, like the poor souls whom the *unterwachtmeister* had intended to execute. Livingston himself didn't know what he'd do with the two German soldiers at the factory. But this . . .

There was cruelty evident in the nakedness of the corpses. It was a final insult, to be stripped before they were hanged. He stopped below a young man who looked like Andrei. This had to be Leonid. The Germans obviously didn't spend much time questioning him. He'd been executed quickly because, in a day or two, it wouldn't matter what the Russians were planning or where they were hiding. In a day or two, they'd all be dead.

It occurred to Livingston, then, that that was why the Germans wanted the men in the tunnel taken alive. They were to be added to this gallery. Probably photographed, their portraits sent back to the Führer.

As Livingston walked, he noticed a ladder propped behind the box office of a movie theater. Opening it, Livingston moved down the street, untying each of the bodies. His fingers were numb, his eyes grew bleary from the storm, but it didn't matter. Nothing mattered, save for giving these tragic souls a final measure of dignity.

When he finally returned to the factory, he found Colon waiting for him.

"The Reds at the river told me where you went," he said, then cocked a thumb at the two soldiers. "How come these *organi* are still alive?"

Livingston walked over to the Germans. "That's a damn good question." In German, he asked, "How in God's name could you people *do* something like that?"

The soldier said nervously, "General P–Paulus said it would be an—object lesson. The general s–said it would cause the Russians to leave the city."

Livingston pulled out his gun. "Do you really believe that *crap*? Has it deterred a single damn Russian?"

"I—I don't *know*."

"Did you put any of those people there yourself?"

"No—"

Livingston put the gun under the Germans' nose.

"*Yes!* Two or three—*please*! They said it would send the enemy . . . a *message*!"

"And maybe it'll send a message to *your* countrymen if I leave the two of you hanging outside with big holes in your goddamn heads!"

"*Nein!* We had no choice!"

"You *had* a choice. What you don't have is *guts*."

The soldier said nothing more and tried not to shake. He failed. Livingston saw tears in his eyes. The other German was staring ahead, resigned to his fate.

Putting away the Luger, Livingston faced one of the Russians. He pointed toward the theater, to the captives, then made a shoveling motion.

"Take these bastards out to bury your people. Wait until tonight, if you have to, until it's clear." He pointed to the Germans, made a running motion with his fingers. "When they're finished, let them go."

"*Svabodni?*" a woman declared, turning an imaginary key.

"Yes. Free them."

The Russians were clearly unhappy. Livingston said, "You *must* do it. Let them go back and tell the others that *you* are not animals. Make the general think about what *they've* become."

Colon said, "He'll care?"

Livingston turned slowly. "*I* care. After what I just saw, it matters what *we* do."

Though the Russians didn't understand his words, they seemed to grasp his meaning. After talking among themselves, they nodded.

The lieutenant faced the Germans. "Tell your general what the people here are made of. Tell him they don't need to resort to barbarism to keep their home."

There was a smugness, a glow in the bright blue eyes of the gagged soldier. A small, crescent scar on his left cheek rose slowly as he smiled beneath the gag. He obviously knew about the gas.

Livingston grabbed the man by his jacket. "Smile, you cocky bastard, but you and your comrades are in here for the long haul. I'm going to see to that *personally*."

Releasing the man, Livingston stormed outside. Colon joined him, raising his collar against the storm.

"You should've plugged him, sir. He ain't worth getting your bowels in an uproar."

"That's all right, anger keeps me warm. Besides, I had to have my say."

"Frankly, sir, I liked your first idea best. We should've taken 'em out and hung 'em up headless. T'hell with moralizin'. *That* would've scared the crap outta the other Krauts."

After returning to the factory to bid the Russians farewell, the Americans set out.

"Ten o'clock," he snarled. "Even time moves like it's made of ice here."

To lessen the chance of being fired at by Russian snipers, Livingston followed the same route Ogan and Andrei had taken. However, he hadn't expected to run into them outside the city.

There was no chance to avoid the men: Livingston and Colon turned around a bluff just as the German squad came from the opposite direction.

When he saw Andrei with his hands raised at the head of the squad, and Ogan in the middle, beside the *oberwachtmeister*, Livingston felt like he had when they'd paddled across the river. They were trying to go one way, but the current kept taking them another.

None of the men acknowledged each other as they passed. However, as Livingston and Colon passed the squad leader, the German stopped.

"Those men's shoulder straps," the NCO said to Ogan. "I thought you were the only one who survived the battle."

Livingston glanced back, saw Ogan hesitate. *Deny us!* he screamed inside. *Tell him we must have stolen the damn uniforms!*

But Ogan said nothing, and the NCO drew his gun. "I had a feeling about you." He yelled to his men, "Take them *all*!"

Because their clothing was so bulky, Livingston and Colon had been carrying their rifles rather than wearing them slung over their shoulders. Thus, before Livingston or Colon could move, three Karabiners and two pistols were leveled at them. Slowly, they put their hands on their heads.

The *oberwachtmeister* looked at each of the men. "You're not even German!" He scowled at Colon.

"Thank God," Colon said in German, and spat. The butt of a rifle came down on the back of his neck and dropped him to his knees.

"Since you seem so anxious to be heard," said the squad leader, "we'll start with you. Who are you and why are you here?"

Colon raised his face and spit again. This time the *oberwachtmeister* kicked him, and growling, Colon scrambled to his feet. The rifle brought him down again, and one of the soldiers put his boot on Colon's neck.

"You goose-stepping blue-eyed *porco*—"

The NCO took the rifle from the soldier and clubbed Colon twice in the side of the face. Livingston ran at him and a soldier kicked him in the gut. The lieutenant doubled over.

"Pick him up," the *oberwachtmeister* ordered. Livingston was pulled to his feet. "We will go someplace it's warm, and maybe you'll think more clearly. If not— I assure you, it will be a most unpleasant day for you all."

He ordered Livingston to help Colon, and as the men were marched back into the city, toward the German-occupied sectors, Livingston saw something that made his heart sink even further.

A German company had moved in and surrounded the factory. Their footprints in the snow told the story. They had come to the tunnel, found the dead soldiers, and followed the tracks made by the Russians, Colon, and him.

The Russians had a few pistols. The Germans would have submachine guns. The Germans in the factory would be killed—if not by the Russians, then by their own people—and so would the Russians. If only he hadn't told them to stay . . .

In six years of fighting, Livingston had never experienced anything approaching the desolation he felt now. His only hope was that Lambert and Weyers would stop the boats, Masha would somehow stop the train, and winter would finish what the invaders had started. . . .

Leaving the South African behind, Lambert went to the bunker. Weyers watched as the wiry Frenchman strode ahead, bent low so that his chest was nearly touching the snow. However, something to the right caught Lambert's eye and, suddenly, he turned from his path and headed toward the Volga. Creeping from the woods, Weyers looked toward the river and saw two soldiers standing at a pier, guarding several barrels of oil and a pair of four-man motorized assault boats.

Weyers hurried ahead and joined his friend. When he arrived, the Frenchman pointed to one man. Sneaking up behind them, Lambert pushed that man into the river and held his head underwater, while Weyers broke the other man's neck.

That part was clean and simple. So was hiding their bodies under the pier, using their belts to lash them to the pilings. However, Weyers was surprised when Lambert kept both of their machine guns, one tucked under each arm.

"What are you doing?"

"Carry over one of these barrels for me," Lambert said. "Open it near the chimney, pour some in, and then run *comme l'enfer.*"

"Run like hell?"

"Into the woods. And stay there."

Now Weyers began to worry. "Rotter, what are *you* going to be doing?"

"Standing right here, making sure none of them gets away."

"Gets away? Half the *shore's* going to vanish when this blows. *No one* will get out of there alive!"

"And if *one* man does? How do we know it wasn't *he* who killed our friends? Hurry, Wings, before one of them comes out to piss."

Muttering under his breath, Weyers tilted the great, black barrel onto an edge and began rolling it through the snow.

The chimney of the bunker had been hacked in the ledge, a pan-size hole from which gray smoke rose along with the distinctive smell of burning oak. Bringing the barrel up the hill and down onto the roof, Weyers used his pocketknife to punch two holes in the top of the barrel. Then, digging a small channel in the wet snow, he lay the container on its side. When the first of the oily liquid began oozing down the trough, Weyers ran from the bunker. Right to Lambert's side.

"*Un fou!* What are you doing?"

"Helping you make sure none of them gets away."

Both men dropped to their bellies. The seconds became minutes, and they began to wonder if something hadn't gone wrong.

"It occurs to me," Weyers said, "that if they're using the fire to cook, we're dead."

"*Oui.* And if it's soup, or *rotkohl*, they won't even *taste* the petrol."

There were voices behind the bunker. The snow had stopped, and the two men watched as a pair of soldiers came out for a smoke and fresh air.

Weyers said, "If they come around front, they'll see that the guards are missing."

"I know." Lambert reached into his pocket. "Cover me."

"Why?"

Without answering, Lambert ran toward the bunker. Weyers licked his lips as he stared down at the gunsight. The soldiers were standing just beyond the left wall of the bunker, staring up the hill, away from the river. He was glad, at least, that they were wearing their fur pile caps with the headdresses that covered their ears. It was unlikely they'd hear Lambert.

Just then, one of the men pointed down. They'd noticed Weyers's footprints. The South African wriggled his body back and forth, tried to get as low in the snow as possible. He continued to watch as the Frenchman, instead of attacking the men, grabbed the roof ledge in front of the bunker and pulled himself up. Weyers prayed the fuel didn't blow up *now*.

A match flared in Lambert's hand. He cupped his hand behind the flame, set a handkerchief on fire, and dropped it down the chimney. Then he spun and dove from the ledge.

There was a very small explosion as the oil dripping down the chimney ignited. The roof lifted up slightly with a muffled roar, then collapsed back down, snow and rock cascading inward, toward the heart of the blast. The barrel was among the last of the debris to fall, but fall was all it did. Snow from the ledge had extinguished the fire, and it failed to explode.

Weyers jumped to his feet and ran forward. He shot the two men who had been standing out back, then stopped to cover Lambert, who had stopped running. Men were coughing and helping others from the wreckage, and Lambert was gunning the men down as they emerged. Holding his own machine gun waist high, Weyers kept a sharp watch for anyone who wasn't killed by Lambert's fire; the South African didn't have to shoot again.

When there was no longer any movement or sound, the two men cautiously approached the bunker from opposite sides.

The carnage had been complete. A few bodies had been torn apart by the blast, but the bulk of the men—at least twenty of them—had been gunned down.

"Tres bien," Lambert said as he surveyed the damage. He poked among the dead men, seemed to be searching for something. Suddenly, a look of triumph crossed his features.

"Voilà!" He held up a pack of cigarettes. "They are Abel's! These pigs did the killing, all right. I feel very good about this—very good indeed."

Lambert lit one of the cigarettes, blew out smoke—and lost it as Weyers grabbed him and pulled him behind the tree. A heartbeat later, the ruins erupted in a massive fireball. The tree was sheared just above their heads, and other trees, nearer the blast, were uprooted entirely. It rained particles of the bunker and ground for nearly a minute.

When the dirt, rocks, snow, flesh, and pieces of uniform had settled, Lambert shook off the debris and stood.

"Mon Dieu, how did you know?"

"I saw black smoke, and figured the petrol drum was finally smoldering."

Lambert looked back toward the wreckage. "It's good that you did, *mon ami.* These bodies seem much thinner than before." Lambert began pacing then, suddenly lost in thought. "But you know, this has given me an idea about how to deal with the boats."

"Really?"

"Yes." Lambert headed toward the river. "Come with me, we have much to do before our friends arrive."

Chapter Nine

The four men were marched to a largely undamaged office building, which served as a field headquarters for the advance units of the Sixth Army. There, they were turned over to *Generalleutnant* Edmund von Horstenau, and taken to a boiler room in the basement. Beneath the glow of a single bare bulb, the men were stripped to the waist, their hands bound behind their backs, their legs tied together; their legs were also tied to iron hooks that had been set in the floor. A rope was loosely tied to each man's throat and hung down his back. Behind them stood a burly soldier who, apart from the *generalleutnant,* was the only other man in the room.

Horstenau paced the small concrete chamber, ignoring the occasional roar of the large, iron burner behind them. There was an ivory cigarette holder in one hand and a short length of hose in the other. He put the holder between his teeth.

"You three are English. Or American perhaps?" His dark eyes were like little cameras, growing wide and narrowing as he studied Livingston, Ogan, and Colon in turn. When he reached Andrei, the lieutenant general sneered. "We know what *you* are, Russian dirt. Do you understand me? Do you speak a civilized tongue, animal?'' Andrei said nothing and the officer looked at the other men. "I expect stubbornness from this mindless thing, who shall hang in any event. But I have no desire to hang you alongside him. Cooperate with me, and you will be sent to a prisoner-of-war-camp outside Leningrad. You will be cared for until the Reich is victorious.'' He approached Ogan, stared at him down his long, slender nose. "*You* are English. You have that . . . look. That air of righteousness.'' He tapped one of Ogan's fingers with the hose. "And I see you are married. Do you want to make your bride a widow?'' He dragged the hose repeatedly along his chin, then along his groin. "Or we can arrange it so that she will have to turn to other men for satisfaction. Which will it be, English? Pain? Or will you tell me how many others were sent in with you, and where they are now?''

Ogan said nothing, and Horstenau smiled around his holder.

"As you wish. Hang for a lost cause.'' He walked over to Livingston. "And you? Will you talk or die?''

"My name is Livingston. Lieutenant. Serial number—''

The German brought the hose across Livingston's neck. He fell to his side, his teeth clenching as he landed on his shoulder.

The officer smiled. "You see? It's a simple but effective means of persuasion. The blow hurts, but not nearly as much as being unable to break your fall.''

The officer nodded to the man in back, who came forward immediately, grabbed the rope attached to Livingston's neck, and pulled him to his feet.

The officer went to Colon. "You spit at the *oberwachtmeister*. Do you have the courage, now, to stand alone again—to be wiser than your comrades?''

"*Kussen* my butt,'' Colon replied.

The German frowned. "Butt?'' he repeated the English. Then he smiled, clapped once. "*Butte!* I see.''

The smile remained as he undid Colon's trousers. "Yes, I will be happy to oblige you."

The pants dropped to the floor, followed by Colon's shorts, and the officer stepped behind him. The hose slashed across him; Colon gasped and his legs trembled, but he didn't fall.

"Admirable. But before we are finished . . . *kissing*, you will scream. *And* you will talk."

Andrei and Ogan continued to stare ahead, but Livingston watched as the officer beat Colon. The private dropped to his knees after the third blow, and was pulled up by the noose; he fell again on the fourth blow, his face striking the ground and leaving a smear of blood when the big soldier yanked him to his feet. Livingston watched to keep his hate strong. If a miracle occurred and he had an opportunity to strike back, he didn't want to do what he'd done at the factory; he didn't want any feeling that was remotely human to get in his way.

The beating lasted for twelve blows. When it was finished, Colon somehow managed to climb to his knees, and then to his feet. His entire lower back and the upper part of his thighs were bloody and raw; there were deep gashes on his forehead and chin.

But he stood, and when the lieutenant general came around from behind, Colon stared flush into his eyes, spit blood at him, and wheezed, "Kiss it again, f–faggot."

Horstenau's eyes narrowed and widened furiously. Slapping Colon's jaw hard with the hose, he lifted his chin with a finger. "I will, young man, I promise. Right before we hang you in the gallery."

He stepped back from the men. "I will return in a half hour, *meine Herren*. Use that time to consider carefully what you will say then. If one of you tells me what I wish to know, all but the Russian will be spared. Otherwise, thirty-three minutes from now, you will all be hanging from lampposts, food for the dogs."

The Germans left, and as soon as the iron door shut, Colon fell to the ground, unconscious. Livingston lowered himself to his knees and backed toward him. The private's head was close enough so that he was able to reach his temple.

"His pulse is strong," the lieutenant said. "The guy's made of iron."

Ogan sat heavily, his legs folded under him. "That won't help when they take us outside. What do you suppose the 'gallery' is?"

Livingston told him, and when he was finished, the Englishman's features were dark. "From the people who brought you the Blitz, another innovation in the art of war."

"More innovative than you think," Livingston said. "When I cut the bodies down, I saw a generator at the other end of the street. Scarce as fuel is, the sons of bitches actually use the street lamps to light the bodies at night."

While he was speaking, Livingston stood and tried to wriggle his wrists free of the ropes.

"I tried that while our friend was whacking Colon," Ogan said. "They won't give."

Livingston stopped and looked around. "There's got to be *something* we can do!"

"We can always spoil his fun by hanging ourselves," Ogan said only half in jest, eyeing the noose around Livingston's neck.

Livingston looked from the Englishman to Colon. "You know, there may be something to that."

"What, suicide?"

"No. The ropes."

Livingston dropped down and backed over to Colon. He was able to reach the knot around his neck, and began to work on it."

"What are you going to do if you get it?"

"Loop it through the metal hook."

"And?"

"Pass one end to you, and one end to Andrei so the two of you can pull. Look, the damn things aren't cemented there, they're just hammered in. If I can get the hook free, I can come over and try to undo your hands."

Pulling frantically at the knot, Livingston was able to work a finger into one of the loops, and managed to undo the knot. He sat down, passed the rope through the iron hook, then maneuvered to each end in turn. With a small flick of his bound wrists, he passed one end to Ogan; Andrei, however, was too far.

"Never mind. I may be able to do it myself." Livingston reeled in the rope and grabbed it tightly behind him. "Ready?"

Ogan nodded, and leaning forward, both men pulled upward so the rope formed a V, with the hook in the center.

"No good," Livingston said, "there's too much slack."

"Let me see what I can do," Ogan said, sliding the rope through his own hook in order to gain some added tension. The men began pulling again; ironically, it was Ogan's hook that eventually gave.

"The weakest link," Ogan muttered as he hopped over to Livingston. Backing up so they were hand to hand, he began working on the lieutenant's wrists.

Moments later, Andrei was beside them, his hands free. Ogan and Livingston stared at him.

"What the hell did you do?" Ogan asked.

Andrei allowed himself a rare smile. He held up his forearms, made two fists. His wrists expanded to nearly twice their normal size.

"Slipped out," Livingston said. "Incredible."

"*Nyet* incredible," Andrei said as he stopped and began pulling the ropes from the lieutenant's feet. "Houdini."

Ogan and Andrei picked up Colon and lay beside the

burner, where it was relatively warm. Then Livingston went to the door and examined the lock.

"I don't suppose you can handle this too, Andrei."

The Russian shook his head.

Ogan rubbed his bare arms. "It wouldn't matter, really, sir. We'll need clothes and arms if you plan to leave the building. The only way we're going to get guns is when the lieutenant general comes back."

Livingston nodded, and the three men went over to the burner to stay warm. The lieutenant found a rag lying over a pipe, and used it to clean Colon's wounds; then, restless, he went and stood by the door. However, as he waited for the Germans to return, what he heard was not at all what he'd expected to hear.

Early in June 1941, as part of the ill-fated French Sixth Army, Lambert had fought the Germans on the Seine. The battle for France had been all but lost by then. Troops had been surrendering all along the front, and the Italians had declared war against the French, joining the German invasion.

Along with refugees from the Fourth and Seventh Armies, Lambert had formed a guerilla group that proved effective for several weeks, harassing the southward-moving Germans along their flanks. With the fall of France, Lambert had joined de Gaulle's Free French Forces in London, where he'd remained until he was recruited by Force Five.

The defense of the Seine had been unmemorable, largely because so many troops were ordered to retreat rather than attempt a defense. The few companies like his own that did make a stand had been quickly decimated and forced to scatter. However, Lambert had been particularly troubled because, when there was still time to mount an offense, his commander hadn't allowed him to try a plan he'd worked out with several other Foreign Legion veterans.

"We can *stop* them!" he'd told Captain de Chagney in his tent. "They won't bother to search the riverbed!"

The elderly officer had huffed, "You've only fought in the desert, Lambert. I won't trust the fate of twenty-two divisions to your plan!"

"What about the fate of *Paris*? If the enemy crosses here, the city will be theirs!"

But the captain had been too busy to listen, too busy loading his staff car with maps and reports. The city had fallen, and de Chagney, along with most of the ex-Foreign Legionnaires, had died when the surviving French troops were surrounded, divided, and gunned down outside of Chartres.

Lambert's plan had been simple, and he'd been aching to try it ever since: to place petrol tanks underwater and, when the German army was well into the river, shoot holes in the containers and set the fuel afire.

Not that the situation on the Volga was exactly the same. Though they could start a fire that would stop the ships, it might not sink them. In that case, each man would get on board one of the vessels by posing as survivors of the bunker blast. They'd found sticks of dynamite buried in a concrete-reinforced pit in the bunker; going below, they'd sink the ships using the explosives. Lambert calculated that one stick fore and one aft would be sufficient to drown each boat without rupturing the tanks.

"And if they don't believe there are still partisans in the woods?" Weyers asked. "If they think *we* started the fire?"

"Two men doing so much damage? *C'est absurde!* Trust me, Wings, nothing will go wrong."

"Trust you! The last time you said that was before we left for Algiers, when you were sure that bloke wouldn't find you with his wife. How close did he come to blowing your head off?"

"That was a fluke. On occasion—on very *rare* occa-

sion—a beautiful woman will blind me. But never a Nazi.
They are not only as unpleasant as rain, they are as pre-
dictable.''

Weyers still wasn't convinced, but as he had no other
plan, he agreed to Lambert's proposal.

The first order of business was to collect pieces of
wood from the bunker, then dry them using swatches of
the dead men's uniforms. Fortunately, the outpost had
been a typical field facility, and the men found sufficient
remnants of wooden tables and chairs for the job. They
lit a fire outside, staying close to it as the noon sun failed
to make its presence felt. There was also, Lambert was
glad to see, a powerful transmitter. When they were finished drying the wood, he found the twisted remains of
its antenna, yanked off the wire, and began winding it
around his arm.

''*Zut!* Only twenty meters' worth.''

Weyers held up a length of wire. ''Here's more we can
use.''

''That's another ten meters or so. We need at least
forty for two separate lines.''

''There are hammocks. Can we knot them together—''

Lambert shook his head. ''The colors are too light.
Lookouts on the boats may see them.'' The men began
lifting slabs of stone and wood. ''Not even a length of
clothesline, or nylons for the women. What kind of army
do these people run anyway?''

''The kind with supply lines stretched thin as a Scot's
shilling,'' Weyers said.

Lambert kicked a shattered chair, then stared out at
the river as the winds caused eddies of snow to dance
across the banks. ''Well, we'll only be able to cover the
middle of the river. We'll weight the ends of the wires
with stones to hold them in place, then hide on opposite
shores with a drum or two apiece. If the convoy tries to
sneak around, we can dump oil in the gap before we go
aboard.''

Weyers agreed, and bringing the materials to shore, they began knotting what Lambert dubbed "Le Maginot en Miniature"—though as Weyers was quick to point out, if it didn't stop the Germans any better than its big brother had in France, they and Stalingrad both would be finished.

Chapter Ten

There was shooting from somewhere outside the boiler room.

Livingston had placed his ear to the door, wincing as the cold burned his flesh. The gunfire was several blocks away, but Livingston liked the sound of it: not just Lugers and German 98ks, but Russian Sudarevs as well. When the Germans attacked the factory, the Russians must have counterattacked near here; he felt a welling of satisfaction at the courage and simplicity of the strategy.

Fired by the Russian assault, Livingston set Ogan and Andrei to the task of trying to dismantle the boiler. A worn, black brute of a tank, it had a pair of rusted iron pipes and a cross-pipe jutting H-like from the top. Ogan pulled the bent hook from the floor and began scraping at the joints where the center pipe was attached to the others; Andrei lashed one of the ropes around it and pulled each time Ogan scratched away. The quarter-meter-long pipe wouldn't be much of a weapon, but it might be something they could use to work off the hinges of the door.

It was a long shot, but that wasn't the point. Livingston didn't want his men sitting around. If the battle came this far, he wanted them to be on their feet, ready for action.

Andrei hadn't asked about his brother, and Livingston hadn't offered any information. Perhaps the Russian assumed Livingston hadn't learned anything. Perhaps he hoped to find him here. Perhaps he simply didn't want to have his worst fears confirmed.

Andrei continued tugging at the pipe. There was a groan. *"Predityeh!"* the Russian barked.

Ogan hurried over and continued scraping at the joint. "It's going to give! *Pull!*"

Livingston came over and grabbed the rope. He wrapped a length around his wrists and braced his heels against the boiler. He and Andrei pulled in unison, and the corroded iron snapped. Thin wisps of steam entered the room through the break, showing the feeble way the boiler had been warming the building. Ogan immediately climbed on top of the tank and put his shoulder to the bar. It bent up, he pulled it down, and he pushed it up again. The rusted iron gave easily, and Ogan handed the length of pipe to Livingston. Stomping down on one end, he flattened it, then used it like a crowbar to try to loosen the hinges.

As he pried at the bolts, he could hear the gunfire getting closer. There were muffled shouts: German voices from just outside the building. Then he heard Russian voices. They seemed a bit farther—

Footsteps and gunfire sounded on the stairwell, along with more German voices. The Germans were retreating! There was nothing downstairs but the boiler room. They were going to have to come in here for cover.

"Ogan! Andrei! Over here, quickly!"

The men abandoned the boiler as Livingston directed them to positions around the room. He gave Andrei the pipe and positioned him right beside the door. Colon, just regaining consciousness, was moved to safety behind the boiler, while Ogan crouched on the other side of the door with a length of rope. After smashing the light, Livingston squatted beside Andrei with the other end of the rope.

The gunfire had reached the door. Keys clattered in the lock. The door swung in.

Rifles and pistols firing, three Germans backed in. They were unaware of the darkness and saw neither Andrei nor the rope Ogan and Livingston suddenly pulled taut behind them, knee level. Andrei swung the pipe and one soldier flew from the room, his skull shattered, while the other two tumbled over the rope. One of them was Horstenau.

Livingston jumped on the *generalleutnant* and Ogan fell on his companion.

"Welcome back, you miserable sonofabitch," Livingston said through his teeth. He rose and snatched the pipe from Andrei. "Here's a kiss *you'll* never forget!"

Livingston swung the pipe like a golf club; the German's head snapped viciously to the side. Ogan dispatched the other man with two blows square in his nose. Then the prisoners rose and peered through the smoke of the gunfire.

Four Russians stormed into the cellar, a tall, slender woman in the lead. They took up positions behind a filing cabinet and the banister; when there was no return fire from the boiler room, they rose slowly.

"Force Five?"

Before Livingston could answer, Andrei bolted through the doorway. "Masha?"

The woman handed her submachine to one of the men behind her. Running over, she embraced her brother tightly.

"Andrei," she said softly.

After a moment, she stepped back and touched his cheek. Unsmiling, she began speaking to him quietly. Livingston heard Leonid's name mentioned; from Andrei's darkening expression, he knew that she'd seen the bodies in the gallery.

When she was finished, Andrei turned and went to the corner beside the boiler.

Masha faced the others. Looking at her now, Livingston could see that she was considerably older than her brother, at least in her early thirties. She had dark eyes and long, black hair streaked with white dust. Her parka was old and ragged and also covered with powder.

"I am Masha Vlasov," she said in thickly accented English. "Are you Livingston?"

"I am. Thank you for coming."

"You are fortunate. We used the tunnel to get to the factory, where we hoped Andrei would be waiting with you. Those who were there had seen you led away, told us what happened." Her voice grew hard. "When the Nazis arrived, they volunteered to stay behind, draw the enemy to them, so we could come and get you."

Livingston looked down. "I wish I could thank them."

"You can, Livingston. Help me stop the train, and they will not have died needlessly." Her eyes softened slightly. "Tell me. Was it one of you who cut Leonid and the others down?"

Livingston said that he had done it, and Masha thanked him sincerely. "All is not black," she said. "There are, yet, those who have honor."

The other Russians introduced themselves. Sergei was a brute of a man who was nearly as wide as he was tall; Piotr was as gangly a man as Livingston had ever seen. But their eyes burned with purpose, and he felt good knowing what they were on his side. The Russians offered the men their coats, but, thanking them, Livingston said that their own German uniforms might serve them better.

While the three men recovered their clothes from a corner of the room, one of the Russians stripped the *generalleutnant* and gave his uniform to Andrei. At first, the young Russian refused to put it on; only after a few strong words from his sister did he relent.

As Livingston pulled on his coat, he asked Masha what the situation was with the train.

"It is not good. The Germans have stopped, for now, to repair a small section of track we destroyed well outside the city. But the cars are heavily armored, and there are soldiers on board the train—at least sixty. We did not have people or arms sufficient to take it."

"That means the boats are probably carrying a few companies as well."

"How many men did you send there?"

When Livingston told her, the woman's expression soured. "Two! What can two men do against a convoy?"

"Probably more than two dozen. All along, it was our plan to get on board *somehow*. An all-out attack against a convoy, speeding upriver, would have been useless."

Ogan came over. "Don't worry. They're extremely able men."

"Let's worry about the train," Livingston said. "How long until it gets moving again?"

"Tonight, perhaps. Very early."

"And how long until it reaches the terminal?"

"Tomorrow, I would guess. Early in the morning. The Germans will be moving slowly, to watch out for sabotage along the track."

"What's the terrain like in between?"

"Mostly flat. A few hills—and one bridge, just outside the city."

"How high?"

"Ten meters, maybe. But you can't blow it up. If any of the tanks fall from the bridge, they will certainly break."

"And if we attack the train outright," Ogan said, "they'll cut us down. Doesn't sound promising."

"No, it doesn't," Livingston agreed. He took the Karabiner from the unconscious *generalleutnant*. "But we'll worry about that after we've had a look at the train." He walked over to Colon, who was sitting with his back to the wall.

"You look like hell, Private."

"Feel like it too."

"Can you walk?"

With Livingston's help, he struggled to his feet. Wiping blood from his cheek, he went to get his clothes. "Show me a German, sir, and I'll *run* to plug a knife in him."

"Good man," Livingston said.

Dressed and armed, the makeshift unit left the cellar and cautiously made its way to the street. Gunfire could still be heard at the factory, and it took all of Livingston's self-control not to go and help the beleaguered Russians. The temptation clearly tore at Masha and her countrymen as well. However, they all understood that the survival of the city came first and, bent low and staying to deserted side streets, the group cautiously picked its way around the fighting, heading toward the northern end of the city, the terminal, and the tracks beyond.

"It figures," Weyers moaned. Only one of the two assault boats started, and they'd planned on having two to deploy the wire.

"Lousy German industry!" Lambert said. "Just make sure *this* one doesn't fail, or we'll have real problems."

While Weyers ran the engine, Lambert doffed his boots and three layers of socks and waded into the river. It was the only place where the rocks weren't frozen to the ground. After fetching an armful, he raced back to shore. Dropping the stones beside the boat, he held his bare feet over the smoking, rattling engine.

"I swear, monsieur, I would rather be in *hell* than in a place which has winter."

"Hey—if your plan doesn't work like you say, you may get your wish."

"It will work, Wings. Next time, I think I'll take my-self a partner who doesn't *doubt* so much."

Weyers snorted. "Yeah, I can just see you and Colon. You'd kill each other inside of two minutes."

Satisfied with the engine, Weyers checked the fuel tank, swivel bracket, screws, and drive shaft of the mo-tor, making sure they were free of ice. With one boat running smoothly, Weyers went to the other. The engine still wouldn't turn over, and he performed the same cleanup of ice and mud. When it still didn't start, he stood back.

"Is it beyond repair?" Lambert asked.

"I could search the rubble for tools, if you think that's how I should spend my time."

Lambert checked his watch. "The convoy will be here by two o'clock at the earliest. That only gives us three hours. It will be better, I think, if we concentrate on our preparations."

Weyers stepped into the boat and, after they had soaked the wood with oil, he chugged out into the river. The Frenchman lay one rock-weighted end of the line in the water, some fifteen meters from shore. As the South Af-rican motored across, Lambert fed the wire and wood into the river. The current bent it into a gentle arc, but the line held. They came to within twenty meters of the opposite shore before it played out.

Lambert put his face to the river and said gleefully, "We've *got* them, *mon ami. Regardez!* The waters on either side are too shallow for a corvette or frigate."

"That's fine, but what if they try to run the block-ade?"

"They won't risk burning and sinking. And for all they know, there are partisans waiting to shoot them as they go through."

"But if they *do* run it?"

Lambert made a face. "Then we signal them to stop and take us aboard. While they're busy navigating through the fire, we'll give them a little water to think about."

Weyers picked at a callus. "I still say it's got as much chance of working as a fisherman in the Sahara."

"Be *optimiste*! If nothing else, we'll be warm before we die."

Weyers frowned as they turned back to collect the oil drums. There were nine in all: They put four along the eastern side of the river, where Lambert would be stationed, and five on the far side, where Weyers would be. They hid them all behind mounds of snow, and punctured the tops, just to be ready.

The men were finished just after one o'clock. Lambert left Weyers on the western shore, with instructions to light the line as soon as the convoy was in sight. The ships would stop—and Lambert, waiting downriver in the boat, would deploy the second line behind them and set it ablaze. The men would then dump the remaining oil and set it on fire, after which Lambert would collect Weyers. If the convoy didn't go down, they'd go on board.

It was nearly three o'clock when Weyers saw lights far down the river. For over two hours, he'd sat on the ground, feeling like Lambert as he thought of nothing but the cold, each minute passing with awful, numbing slowness. He wished he could light the dynamite, watch it explode, just to have something to do. The lights were a godsend, and the instant he saw them, he jumped to his feet.

Grabbing the box of matches in his coat pocket, he headed to the bank, crouched behind a rock, and watched the convoy's progress. A horn sounded from the lead boat: two blasts, then silence. The lights continued to near; then there were two more blasts.

Suddenly, the lights slowed. It was a straight run of river; there was no reason for caution.

"C'mon, ya Jerry blighters, what the hell's wrong?"

The lights stopped. There were two more blasts from

the ship's horn, and with a jolt, Weyers realized what
they were doing: signaling the bunker and waiting for a
return blast, an all-clear.

How could we have been so goddamn stupid?

Thinking back, Weyers recalled that somewhere in the
wreckage he'd seen a hand-cranked siren, like the one
the boats were using. The bunker was on Lambert's side
of the river. Did he know it was there? Would he even
think of going to get it?

Weyers dismissed the idea of lighting the fires now;
they might burn out before the enemy arrived. The only
thing to do was to get to Lambert and regroup. It was
some thirty meters across, and he felt that he could survive the cold, could fight the current. What choice did
he have? Rising, Weyers hurried across the shingle and
slogged into the river.

At once, the fabric of his coat and trousers began to
soak up water. Each step became more difficult, and
Weyers was soon forced to strip both garments off. The
frigid water stung his legs, shot through his cotton cavalry shirt, and burned his chest. Up to his neck in the
rushing river, he writhed in torment as he walked. Then,
when he was barely halfway across, his legs went numb
and seemed to vanish from beneath him. Going under,
he twisted with the flow, screaming from the shock of
the cold closing in around him. Water flooded his mouth
as he went down, and his last thought was that this had
been the stupidest plan in which he had ever taken
part. . . .

Chapter Eleven

Livingston didn't know quite what to make of Masha.

Unlike Andrei, who alternately brooded and sobbed about his brother, Masha said nothing. Her expression was unchanging—the eyes remained hard, the mouth straight and stern. When she spoke, her voice was even, without emotion. He didn't understand how anyone could keep so much pain inside.

Before the afternoon had passed, he learned just how she dealt with her sorrow.

It was nearly one, when many of the patrols rested for lunch, and Masha was leading them through a section of town that had once been a pleasant residential area of three- and four-story apartment buildings. Most of the building fronts were still standing, many because they were propped up by the rubble of their fire-gutted interiors. The group was sticking close to the facades, listening for voices or gunfire, when enemy soldiers entered the street from the other side. Livingston's men sunk into doorways, alleys, or behind steps. The young woman and Piotr ducked inside a building.

Watching from an alley, Livingston saw them scale a pile of debris and make for the enemy position. The lieutenant vaulted a shattered brick wall and hurried after them while the rest of his men opened fire on the unwary Germans. Two soldiers went down at once, and the others took up positions in buildings and behind telephone poles, street lamps, and trees.

Behind the buildings, Masha and her companion moved quickly and quietly, the woman exhibiting catlike grace and balance as she climbed over and around debris. She remained in the lead as they approached the last mound of rubble; as a result, she was the first to see the potato masher when it was hurled from the other side.

"Get down!"

Masha screamed as she flung herself behind half a bathtub lying nearby. Livingston dropped to his belly behind her and covered his head. Shrapnel clattered against the tub. Livingston and Masha were spared; out in the open, Piotr was not.

Masha opened fire from around the tub, shooting at the mound, and Livingston scrambled ahead on his belly, trying to get closer. A pair of Karabiners appeared, firing blindly over the mound while Livingston approached.

Instead of coming in over the rubble, Livingston backed down the side of the mound and crept around the one that was hiding the Germans. He came in behind them and, kneeling, shot them both in the head. After throwing one of the rifles out to Masha, he took the other and crawled through the adjoining building.

The Germans were clearly visible through the shattered glass of the front windows. Stopping behind a charred sofa, the only piece of furniture in the room, Livingston aimed at the nearest man, and noted where another was standing nearby. Both fell in quick succession, followed by a third and a fourth. Livingston hadn't shot them; Masha had, from behind him.

Livingston made for the shattered front door of the building and, caught in a crossfire between Livingston and his men, the remaining two Germans went down.

And as he stepped into the street, Livingston saw how Masha handled her sorrow.

Her lips tightly shut, expression still neutral, she began beating one of the dead men. Andrei and Sergei said nothing. They went back and checked on their comrade, and after making certain Piotr was dead, laid him on the ground behind the building and covered him over with pieces of brick and concrete. The dead Germans were left where they lay, as a warning to others.

When the men were finished, they waited silently until Masha was done. Her blows were brutal; she kicked, she punched, she used the butt of her gun on the corpse. And when she was finished, she turned and rejoined her comrades—calmly, as though nothing had happened.

"I know how she feels," Colon said as he passed Livingston. Though his speech was slurred, the lieutenant was glad to see that his eyes burned with their old intensity.

The loss of Piotr was sobering, more so because there were only six of them left. As they rested in the back of a bakery, sharing some cheese and chasing rats from the crumbs, Masha said that gathering more people was out of the question. By day, patrols such as the one they'd just encountered fanned out through the city. Avoiding them would be a feat in itself, let alone trying to get to every cellar and cranny where partisans might be hidden.

While they rested, Masha told Livingston a bit more about the train. The flatbed car to which the gas tanks had been chained was sandwiched between the engine and an armored car. The armored car had a turreted 76.2mm gun on top, for long-range firing, and small ports whose metal doors could be opened and used by the soldiers inside. There were seven such windows on each side of the car. There was also an armored caboose and a spare engine in back.

"Sounds like we've got our work cut out for us," Ogan

said. "We're going to have to find a way to get into the engine."

"That's what I've been thinking," Livingston said. "We take the controls and run it backwards, away from the city."

"Right. The engine would certainly be a defensible position."

"But what do we do then?" Masha asked. "We can't hold out forever."

"If we can get to the engine, we don't have to," Ogan said. "In London, Escott calculated that this new, heavy gas will have an effective range of approximately three kilometers. If we capture the train and derail it where the track runs through the farmland, we can open the containers without the gas reaching the city."

"And hold our breaths for a very long time," Colon remarked.

They continued their journey from door to door, stopping at one point when they ran into a sandbag and barbed-wire barricade stretched across a broad avenue. The impasse hadn't been there the day before; Masha guessed that the Germans were trying to seal off roads that led to the railroad station. They tried another street, but soldiers were also in the process of sealing that route.

Masha led them to a small pond nearby, where a stone bridge afforded cover. They ducked behind one of the supports.

"We have two choices," she said. "We can attempt to go through one of these barricades, or we can try to approach the bridge along another, less direct route."

"And crossing that bridge is the *only* way to get us to the tracks?" Livingston asked.

Masha nodded.

"What's the less direct route?"

"An approach from the west side, through the rail yards."

"Is it safer?"

"If the yards are crowded with trains. Otherwise, there will be a lot of open space to cover, and it will depend upon where the guards are standing and which way they are facing. There's a diagram in one of our bunkers. If we're going to try that approach, it would be best to stop and plan it."

"Is the bunker far?"

"A few blocks."

Livingston rubbed his two-day growth of whiskers, then reluctantly approved the stopover. Time was short, but precision in this phase of the operation was also important.

As they moved out—one at a time, around the pond, with Livingston bringing up the rear—the lieutenant was distracted by something that Colon had mentioned before: that several people would have to be close to the gas tanks in order to open them.

Never could he remember ever having worked so hard, and all for the privilege of dying.

When Lambert was certain the convoy was slowing, he used a piece of wood to backpaddle the boat into a clump of reeds. He didn't dare use the engine; the noise or the fumes would have been noticed. Peering through the moss and vines that hung over the water from a gnarled beech tree, he watched as the boats signaled again, then stopped.

Obviously, they weren't going to move until the signal was returned. Even if he had a siren, Lambert had no idea what to send back, whether the convoy expected the same signal, or something different.

He stayed calm, decided it didn't matter. The important thing was to get the fires going, to delay the convoy, to lure a search party over and get on board.

He looked upriver. There was no movement on the shore where Weyers was hidden; it was clear he didn't intend to deviate from the plan. The river was now an enemy. Lambert couldn't yell the change of plans to Weyers and be heard; he couldn't fire his pistol, or the Germans might hear; he couldn't rush over, or the Germans might see.

Suddenly, his concerns became academic as Weyers shot from his cover and splashed into the water.

"What in God's name is he doing? *L'imbecile!*"

The Frenchman watched with horror as Weyers labored through the torrent, tearing off his coat, getting caught in the flow, and going under.

Lambert pulled on the starter cord, but the engine wouldn't turn over. He tried it again, but it still wouldn't start.

Swearing, he jumped from the boat and ran along the bank. As he peered into the dark river, Lambert wasn't even certain he'd be able to see Weyers, let alone save him. Though it was only half-past three, the sun was already low behind the hills, casting long shadows. Any movement on the water's surface could have been the figure of a man.

He raced through the snow, his legs heavy, eyes searching desperately for a sign of his friend.

Then he saw it. A hand sticking up from the water. But it wasn't being carried downriver, and Lambert soon saw why: Weyers had managed to snag the line, and was holding on to it.

Climbing into the second assault boat, which was still moored to the pier, Lambert pulled it back several meters, upstream of where his friend was. When Lambert climbed in, the current carried him toward the line, the Frenchman using the tiller to guide it to the center of the river. He came close enough to Weyers to grab his wrist and, reaching into the river, found his belt and managed to pull him in.

The South African's fingers were bent stiffly around the wire, and it came in with him. As the boat twisted madly downriver, Lambert pinched Weyers's nose shut,

put his mouth to the South African's pale blue lips, and
blew hard. Weyers responded, and a few seconds later
he breathed in again, and then a third time.

After the fourth breath, Weyers stiffened and gulped
down air. Lambert pulled off his coat and wrapped it
around his friend.

"You'll be all right, Wings. Le Rodeur has things
under control."

Patting his friend on the chest, Lambert looked frantically about for something to stop them from being carried toward the convoy. There was nothing in the boat
but the seats, the motor—and the line Weyers had dragged
in. The rocks were still attached to the ends, and though
they weren't heavy enough to serve as an anchor, they
might have another use.

Checking to make sure the wire was tied firmly around
the flat stones, Lambert got to his knees. They were
approaching the beech tree where he'd been hiding and,
swinging the rope over his head, bolo-style, he let one
end go. It caught a branch, but when he attempted to
reel the boat in, the line snapped. Cursing, the Frenchman tried again to turn the engine over. The starter rope
barely drew a sputter.

Swimming for shore was out of the question. Weyers
was nearly blue, and was too large for Lambert to tug
behind him in any case. However, it occurred to Lambert
that they did have *one* chance.

First he had to lighten the boat. Loosening the clamp
screws that held the motor in place, he let it fall back,
then lowered himself over the stern. The water rose to
his chest and the cold shocked him as it had before. But
he was able to skid along the bottom and slow the boat;
at the same time, he began working it sideways, toward
the shore.

It was difficult to breathe, the frigid waters causing his
chest to contract. He stumbled several times, but the boat
steadied him; eventually, the water was only up to his

knees, then his shins. He staggered ashore but didn't stop. Fear kept him going. Afraid someone in the convoy might have seen them, Lambert pulled Weyers from the boat and dragged him up the embankment. He headed for the bunker. Though they were nearly one hundred meters downriver, it was the only hiding place around.

As he struggled ahead, Lambert thought he heard the sound of motors. The frigates had probably lowered launches, sent them to see what the problem was. The men riding them would probably be armed to the teeth.

The sounds grew louder, and were definitely engines. There was no way he'd make it to the bunker before they arrived, and he realized that his tracks, in the snow, would lead the Germans right to him. Panting, his flesh frostbitten, he stopped to try and focus his thoughts, to concentrate.

The boats. The river. The bunker. The dynamite. There was nothing he could use to stop the Germans. With just the one gun, he might be able to hide and snipe at a few of them, but ultimately, they'd prevail. Trying to convince them that they'd survived the bunker attack was out of the question: Weyers was in no condition to surrender on his own, and if they couldn't get into different boats, the plan was useless.

The boats. The river. The bunker—

The dynamite!

Shaking his head violently to try to clear the throbbing pain, Lambert ran ahead. It didn't matter, now, if they knew what he was doing. The important thing was to do it before they could stop him.

Scrabbling the last few meters on all fours, he reached the bunker and, after wrapping himself in the coat of one of the dead men, Lambert went to the reinforced pit. It was out back, away from the bunker in case of fire or attack. Collecting armfuls of dynamite, he started toward the bluff overlooking the river. Realizing he'd left his matches in his coat, he swore, stopped, and began searching the pockets of the dead men. After losing precious minutes, he found a box, then looked back.

Two launches were about two hundred meters from the shore. Lambert cursed again. There was no way he could get up to the cliff, do the job, and get back for Weyers before the Germans arrived. If he went back, he risked not stopping the convoy. If he went ahead, Weyers was a dead man.

He went back.

As he ran, out of breath, he saw the Germans pointing at him. Lighting the fuses, he began heaving the dynamite at the boats. The shallows and the shingle erupted furiously, raising pillars of rock and water. One of the boats was overturned, and those soldiers who weren't killed by the blasts were dragged by the current. The other boat turned and tried to fish the men from the water.

When Lambert reached Weyers, the South African was beginning to come around.

"Very noisy," he whispered.

"Don't . . . add . . . to it," Lambert gasped as he dropped beside him. His legs were weak and trembling. "Can you walk?"

"If not, I can crawl."

"*C'est bien*, because I can't carry you."

Lambert took Weyers's arm and helped him to his feet. The big man took a step, then grabbed Lambert's shoulder for support.

"Sorry, Rotter. Just give me a second." Weyers took several deep breaths, then took a few more steps.

"Let me know when you can stand on your own."

"Why?"

"Because I used up all my explosives. I need to get more."

Weyers told him to go ahead and, his own step uncertain, Lambert left his companion behind.

He had just finished pulling the rest of the dynamite from the pit when Weyers arrived.

"Take these," Lambert said, pushing a bundle of sticks into Weyers's arms.

"And do what? We can't just chuck them at the ships."

"I don't intend to. Just trust me."

Realizing what he'd said, Lambert looked up at Weyers.

"This one *will* work. Whether the ships move or stand still, we've got them."

Their arms full of explosives, the men trudged along the shore. Every muscle in Lambert's body ached, and his head was pounding. But on the bright side, he told himself, at least the convoy hadn't moved, and no other launches had been sent out. Either they had radioed for assistance from a battalion upstream, or were planning to launch a more organized raid. In any case, it gave him ample time for what he had in mind.

The bluffs along this stretch of the Volga weren't as high as they were upriver, the tallest of the crags reaching only some twenty meters. But, like the other cliffs, they were fraught with fissures, caused by eons of water seeping into the rock, freezing, and expanding.

They'd do in the place of a bona fide drill holes.

Once on top, Lambert got on his knees and began burrowing in the snow. Finding a large crack, he traced its course along the length of the cliff. Satisfied, he lined it with TNT, pushing in a stick every meter.

"Going to make like little beavers, are we? If we can't burn the river, we'll dam it."

"Why not, monsieur?"

"No reason. Only, why didn't we think of this in the first place?"

Lambert went back and began packing snow around the base of each stick. "Because it isn't *parfait*. It will stop the ships, but it won't sink the cargo. Hopefully," he said, "we can get to that later."

Convinced that the sticks wouldn't tip over, Lambert stood and fished the matches from his pocket. "Now go. These are short fuses, and a minute after I light them, most of the cliff is going to bid us *adieu.*"

Water had frozen on the South African's lashes. He rubbed it away. "Forget it. I'm staying with you."

"*Non!* There's nothing you can do—"

"Like hell! Suppose you slip and break your goddamn leg? How are you going to get away?" Weyers made an angry face, the dark lines heightened by exposure and exhaustion. "You saved my life, Rotter. In South Africa, that'd make us brothers, and brothers stick together."

Lambert seemed uncomfortable. "*Tres bien,*" he said quietly, "and—thank you."

Striking one of the matches and shielding it from the wind, Lambert touched it to each stick in turn. The fuses hissed wickedly, and when he'd ignited the last of them, the two men turned and ran down the sloping backside of the bluff. When they were nearly to the bottom, the ground heaved violently, a massive pop punched hard at their eardrums, and they threw themselves forward, into the snow. The explosion echoed up and down the river valley, punctuated by the dull thumping of boulders hitting the snow and the noisy rain of dirt and pebbles.

It was nearly a minute before either of them lifted their faces from the snow.

"Rotter, are you all right?"

Lambert had landed hard on his chest and wheezed. "Hitler should feel like I do." He pulled his arms beneath him and sat up. A layer of small stones fell from his back. "This being pelted with rocks—it's getting to be a habit with us."

"Better rocks than bullets."

"*C'est vrai.*" Lambert looked around. Snow was still falling from the blast, a cool, glistening rain that felt good on Lambert's face. After several minutes, the men stood and, making their way through up the bluff, which was now peppered with rocks of all sizes, headed back toward the cliff.

Looking down, Lambert felt as though he'd just won the war. A causeway stretched most of the way across the river. It was uneven, and some of it barely broke the surface, but nothing larger than a rowboat would be able to pass over or around it.

A smile split the Frenchman's cheeks.

"You did it," Weyers said, slapping him on the back. "Damned if you weren't right about *this* one."

"Did you doubt me?"

"Frankly," Weyers said, "I did. Severely." He sat heavily on a jagged slab of rock that had been torn up by the blast. "The question is, what do we do next?"

Lambert sat down beside him. "My guess is they'll try to dig up the dam. When they do, virtually every man will be assigned to the detail. And when that happens, we simply go on board and finish the job we started." Lambert looked back, toward the woods. "As for the immediate future, I suggest we go somewhere, light a fire, dry off, and find something to eat. I've a feeling it's going to be a long night."

Chapter Twelve

Masha, Livingston, and the others left the streets and took to the cellars.

The woman led them through a series of dark basements connected by short, narrow passageways that were little more than rat holes. They stopped to drink in one, where a still-functioning boiler beneath a German outpost had melted the snow and formed one of the few pools that wasn't utterly rank.

The Germans may have claimed to control these areas of the city but, Masha whispered, the Russians had been most effective using these tunnels to make their way behind enemy lines and pick off soldiers.

The cellar network ended under the stage of a music hall. Masha said that she and Andrei knew the building well: Their father used to manage it, and they were aware of crawl spaces and closets the Germans would never find. It was there, in fact, in a scenery pit beneath the stage, that the network of tunnels had been begun. The building hadn't been destroyed because General Paulus admired its beauty, the marble columns outside and bas-relief friezes inside. He vowed that when he took the city, he could make this his headquarters; in a communiqué, Hitler had vowed that he would make Stalin dance on the stage before executing him.

Masha said that she had vowed to raise a new Stalingrad with the nineteenth-century edifice as the centerpiece.

The group emerged beneath the stage and, after making their way through the stacks of furniture and costumes, they were in a basement, facing a life-size portrait of Lenin. The painting swung around in the middle, admitting them to a stairwell that led to a long, narrow room. The walls were brick and the floors were covered with mismatched scraps of carpet.

"It was built by a man who ran this place before my father," Masha said. "He was a czarist, and after the Revolution, my father let him and his family hide until they could escape Russia."

"You come from a long line of heroes," Livingston said.

"Not heroes," she said emphatically, "but lovers—of our people, and of our city."

She lit candles in the room while Andrei went upstairs to stand watch. For the first time since they landed, Livingston felt safe, able to let down his guard. But he couldn't relax. It was two o'clock—less than a day before the gas would be unleashed upon the city.

Masha went to a wooden desk which, along with two small beds and a large washing basin, were the only objects in the room. She took a map of the city from the center drawer and unrolled it beneath a candle. Livingston and Ogan looked down.

"Here are the six roads which lead to the terminal," she said, pointing to them in turn. "Presumably, all are blockaded. Here is the bridge." She used a pencil to sketch the span in profile. "It is an iron trestle, with five supports—one at each end, one in middle, and two halfway between each end and middle."

"How long is it?" Livingston asked.

"Fifty meters."

He looked at the map. "So trains come over the bridge, into the terminal, then down and around under the bridge to the yard where cargo is unloaded."

"Yes."

"And you said the bridge is ten meters high—just enough for trains to pass under into the unloading area." The lieutenant scratched his head. Slats of melting ice fell from the sides. "Do you know anything about running trains?"

"No."

Livingston smiled. "I should have had Weyers stay with us. Sonofagun can run anything." He began pacing. "We have to assume that there will be soldiers all over the place. Which means that even if we get close to the bridge, odds are good that they'll spot us."

"Even if we came through the terminal, they would have seen us," she said. "We'll just have to take our chances."

"Agreed. The question is, can we even get close enough to the damn thing to blow it up? How much do you have in the way of explosives."

"Very little. There is some dynamite in one cache, a bit of petrol, and a few bazooka rockets—but no launcher."

"If what you say about the bridge is true, just a stick of dynamite or two is all we'll need." He stopped his pacing, studied the map intently. "Do you happen to know if the locomotives are coal-driven or electric?"

"They are old steam locomotives."

"Damn."

Ogan looked at the lieutenant. "Why? What did you have in mind?"

"I was thinking that if we could pack one of the locomotives with explosives and move it under the bridge, we could blow the thing to kingdom come. But if the locomotives are all coal-driven, it would have to be stoked—no way we could do that without being seen.''

Ogan pointed to the map. ''Can we come at the bridge from the other side?''

The woman shook her head. ''We'd have to cross the open track. The Germans would see us for certain.''

Livingston continued to stare at the map. ''I wonder—what if a few of us were to launch a diversionary attack from somewhere in the rail yard?''

''While the rest of us do what?'' Ogan asked.

''You said you hid out in a tank before. What was wrong with it?''

Ogan shrugged. ''It was covered with snow. For all I know, it simply ran out of petrol.''

''The German tank on the river?'' Masha asked. ''We clogged the cannon with mud and it split. It's no good to anyone.''

''Maybe it is for us,'' Livingston said. ''Ken—how far upriver was it?''

''About a quarter kilometer.''

The lieutenant looked at the map. ''Masha, what's the best way to get there?''

She thought for a moment. ''Since the Nazis have discovered our one tunnel to the river, the only way is to take the tunnels in the destroyed residential district here, just one block from the back of theater.'' She traced a path with her finger. ''Then go through the park to the river. But there is only open space after the park—very dangerous.''

''We'll have to risk it. Ken and I will go. We'll get the explosives, take the tank, and while you draw fire from the rail yards, we'll ride right up and blow the damn bridge to scrap iron.''

Masha regarded Livingston with a mixture of admiration and disbelief.

''Don't worry,'' the lieutenant said. ''It's a German tank. They'll think we're coming to help.''

"You'll need new clothes," she said. "If you approach the tunnel in those uniforms, there's a good chance you'll be shot before you come within shouting distance."

Ogan said, "There's probably something you can use on the costume rack?"

Colon snickered. "I saw a coupla tutus."

"I meant street clothes."

Livingston said, "We'll check. What about the explosives?" he asked Masha. "Where are they?"

"In a butcher shop, beneath a pile of rotting dogs. Germans will eat raw horseflesh, but not dogs." She allowed herself a rare smile. "We gave up the food to ensure that the weapons would be safe."

Livingston returned the smile, though it was tempered by the knowledge that she was telling the truth.

The group retired to the property room beneath the stage, where the men found civilian clothes. Though they were too large, intended for comedy skits, it was all the men had to choose from.

"It's funny," Masha said when they were finished, "but with clothes too large and torn, and with these caps, you *look* like Russian peasants."

Livingston slid his gun into a shabby overcoat. Despite the condition of the clothes, and the fact that he would be much colder wearing them, he was glad to be out of the German uniform. Now he felt like he was dressed for a fight, not anonymity.

While they dressed, they discussed their timetable. Masha and her people would enter the yards on the western side and begin widespread fire in exactly three hours. At that time, Livingston and Ogan would come from the east with the tank. If for some reason the tank didn't make it, the two men would have to approach the bridge without it. Livingston reminded Masha that even if the gas was released just on the other side of the bridge, fewer Russians would die than if the gas was released in the heart of the city.

"The password is the same?" he asked as they walked toward the backdoor of the theater.

"Yes. I do not know who will be in the tunnels, but a woman named Nona is in command. She will help you."

Livingston and Ogan embraced the Russians.

"You want to hug me too, sir?" Colon asked Livingston.

"Only if you're wearing a tutu."

The private smiled, then wished his companions luck.

Masha checked to make sure there were no patrols outside. When she returned, Ogan and Livingston hurried into the street.

The snow was blinding after the darkness of the theater, and in the courtyard, the two men crouched behind a large, bronze mask of tragedy while their eyes adjusted.

Masha watched them through a peephole her father had installed years before. A strong wind gusted by; when the swirl of snow was gone, so were the men.

It was just before five when, with the last of the daylight to his back, Lambert went to the woods in search of dinner. At once, he spotted two striped squirrels. They were side by side, clutching a tree, facing down and nibbling on snow-covered ivy growing from the trunk. As Lambert raised his gun, the squirrel nearest him looked over, spun, and fled up into the bare branches; the animal behind it looked over, froze, and caught the bullet that was meant for its companion. Blood sprayed across the tree and the animal fell.

"It's like war," he muttered as he trudged ahead. "You took the bullet fate had intended for your buddy."

Not that it mattered to Lambert which squirrel they ate. At this point, it didn't matter whether the squirrel was even cooked. Licking his lips, Lambert ran to fetch the small animal. Unfortunately, Lambert was not alone.

Glancing into the trees, Lambert noticed a wolf standing in the dark shadows. The Frenchman slowed to a walk.

"You go and chase the other squirrel," he yelled. "This one's *pour moi*."

The wolf glowered back at him, its green eyes and gray head moving with Lambert's every step. When the Frenchman reached the squirrel, the wolf voiced a guttural growl.

The Frenchman's palm began to sweat around his pistol. He stared at the wolf and knelt slowly, his eyes never leaving those intelligent, green eyes staring back at him. When Lambert finally gazed down, he frowned.

The blast had decimated the small animal. There was nothing left but the tail and hindquarters, barely enough to serve as an appetizer for—

"Le Loup. Porquoi pas?"

Laying the decimated squirrel on the ground, Lambert smiled as he backed away slowly. . . .

Weyers sat back from the fire he'd made. "I've got to hand it to you, Rotter. I've never eaten wolf." He spit out a chunk of fat. "It's greasy, and there's a lot of gristle, but . . . it's not bad."

"It's better than camel," the Frenchman said. "They taste as bad as they smell."

The South African looked over at the gutted carcass. "Too bad we don't have the time to skin it. The pelt would make very nice gloves or boot lining."

Lambert wiped his hands on his jacket. "Unfortunately, we have to go and see what our friends are up to. How do you feel?"

"The fire's worked wonders, but I can't remember when I've hurt so much *everywhere*."

Lambert noticed the raw, red blisters on Weyers's

hands and, after examining them, lifted Weyers's shirt.
There were huge patches of caked, red skin on his side
and neck.

"Frostbite."

"So?"

"It does not look good."

"What're you talking about? You're a French-Arab
from the desert. You wouldn't know frostbite from a map
of Cape Town!"

"*Peut-etre*. But I do know gangrene, and I'd watch
those spots around your waist and under your arm. They
could become infected."

Weyers pulled down his shirt. "I'll see a bloody doc-
tor on my next day off." He winced as the fabric scraped
his skin. "I'll also take some bandages from the ship's
sick bay if we go on board."

Lambert rose and kicked snow on the campfire. "*Al-
lons*. We've got our half of a city to save."

With a last, longing look at the smoldering embers,
Weyers plucked his coat from an overhanging tree limb
where he'd left it to dry, then followed Lambert to the
bluff.

The Frenchman was surprised to find that not a single
soldier had come to examine the rock slide. The Germans must have concluded that whoever made the strike
had done their job and fled. Lambert looked downriver,
and was also surprised to see that a large force had landed
at the bunker and that the convoy had moved much closer
to it. There were dozens of soldiers standing on the decks
of the two ships, sleek, gray frigates each of which had
a diamond-shaped antenna atop its single mast.

"That's strange," he said.

"What is?"

"Why bother coming just a little farther when they
can't get through?"

The answer came when he heard a deep grinding sound
coming from somewhere behind the rubble of the bun-

ker. The two men listened for nearly a half hour as the
sound came closer. Then, two phalanxes of soldiers appeared, dressed in winter camouflage uniforms. They
were carrying kerosene lanterns, studying the ground for
mines. Between them was a pair of huge, treaded trucks.

"Sweet Jesus Christ," Weyers moaned.

Lambert was silent. The Germans weren't going to
give up. They were going to finish the trip on land.

"We should've sunk the ships when we had the chance,
Rotter."

"*Ca va*. I didn't think they had the stinking *resources*
for this." He stole a look at the skies. "Please, God, let
it snow again."

"Save your prayers for when we need 'em. Those are
Opel Maultiers. Remember the half track we had in Algiers, the one that rode up and over everything? Well,
these are even tougher. Nothing short of a 100mm how-
itzer will stop those treads."

Lambert's mouth went dry. He was oblivious to the
cold, to his battered muscles. All he saw were the trucks
being turned around when they reached the riverbank
while, under the glow of the ship's spotlights, a large
crane at the stern of each frigate began to pivot.

"The bastards are supposed to be out of fuel, Wings.
They don't have enough to run monsters like those."

"Maybe they had just enough. They don't expect to
be here much longer."

Lambert kicked at the snow, then drove a palm against
his forehead. "*Quelle l'ane!* Dammit, *think*! Why is
nothing coming?"

"Because we're both dead on our feet—"

"*Non!* We must think of something, or a *city* will soon
be dead, *period*."

"Can we use more dynamite? Blow up the trucks?"

"We'd never get near them."

"Does that matter, as long as we get close enough to
disable them?"

"It's an option," Lambert said laconically.

"Seems like the only one," Weyers continued. "They have to go through the woods. We could wait there—"

"Wait!" Lambert said. "The woods—*oui*. Something *is* coming to me!" He grabbed Weyers's arms. "Wings, what happened to me before?"

"When?"

"At the lake."

The South African's beefy face twisted in thought. "You mean, when we first got there?"

"*Oui!*"

"You fell."

"And *why* did I fall?"

"Because you didn't—" The South African paused and stared at the Frenchman. Suddenly, the big mouth turned up. "Good God, Rotter—yes. I think you've got something there."

Lambert fired a look back at the bunker. "How long do you think it will take them to load the trucks? An hour?"

"At least."

"And another hour to get through the wood?"

"About that. Those trucks are tough, but they aren't very fast."

"*Magnifique!*"

The Frenchman left the bluff and started back through the woods. Weyers lumbered after him. Lambert was at once delighted—and angry for having doubted himself.

The question now was no longer what they would do to try to stop the shipment. The question was whether they had a chance in hell of succeeding.

Chapter Thirteen

Livingston and Ogan reached the tunnel just after three. Because so many German soldiers had apparently been reassigned to the train and terminal, there were few men about. It was also considerably colder, which Livingston was certain influenced the Germans' will to leave their outposts to patrol.

The tunnel was located in an outhouse. Upon stepping inside, Livingston yelled the password down the hole and waited; in less than a minute, a boy clambered up.

He was no older than fourteen, and there was a German helmet strapped to his head, an old German P.08 tucked in the waistband of his trousers. He spoke no English, but when they asked for Nona, he was able to tell them, through gestures, that she had been killed the night before in a gun battle in the park. In fact, using hand motions, the boy informed them that, after that fight, he was the only one left alive.

Livingston put an arm around his shoulder and commended him. But the boy seemed uncomfortable, making it clear by his posture, by the way he held the gun, that he considered himself a man. The lieutenant understood, and quietly pulled back.

Using his dictionary, Ogan told the youth where they

needed to go and, leading them down the rank hole and
through the tunnel, the boy took them to the butcher
shop. Moving aside the dead dogs—German shepherds,
Livingston was gratified to note—the men found a trapdoor. Opening it, they descended a rickety ladder to a
small basement, where there were five sticks of dynamite, rockets, and a can of petrol.

"Like the woman said," Livingston sighed, "it's not
much."

"If we take the rockets," Ogan suggested, "and abandon the tank when we set the explosives, it'll still cause
a hell of a blast."

Livingston agreed. When they climbed from the small
storage room, the boy made motions that he wanted to
go with them.

"Zdyehs?" Ogan asked.

The boy gestured behind him. *"Zdyehs . . . pa-
tyerya."*

"What'd he say?" Livingston asked.

"I told him that his place was here, but he says that
the battle here is lost."

"Can't really blame him for feeling that way. He had
a hell of a night. Find out his name, Ken."

Ogan asked. "Vladimir," the youth said. "Vladimir
Ilyich Tsigornin."

Livingston offered his hand. "Welcome to Force Five,
Vladimir."

After emerging from the tunnel in a devastated police
station, Vladimir led Livingston and Ogan across the
street to the park.

Like everything else in Stalingrad, the park hadn't been
spared the bombs of the Luftwaffe or the guns of the
Wehrmacht. The iron fence had been shattered, swings
were a mass of broken sticks and tangled chains, and the
benches were overturned or split.

Running around the twisted fence, the men ducked

behind a sandbox, which had been overturned and broken down the middle, forming a pyramid. Trees and debris blocked the opposite side of the park from view; for
all they knew, enemy soldiers might be encamped there.

Indicating that the men should stay where they were,
Vladimir flopped onto his belly and wriggled toward a
kiosk in the center of the park.

Livingston watched as a boy pitted himself against the
threat of battle-seasoned German troops. Vladimir's
courage brought a lump to his throat. Suddenly, the youth
stopped; Livingston heard them too: German voices
coming from somewhere on the other side of the debris.
An engine joined the voices, followed by the clatter of
wood.

Vladimir hurried ahead to the kiosk, then looked back
at the men. He moved his fists as though he were pulling
on a rope.

"They must be setting up a barricade," Ogan said.
"They probably came here after securing the area."

"That figures," Livingston said. "They're probably
looking to contain the Russians in as small an area as
possible before bringing in the gas."

"Do we wait or do we take them?"

"We can't afford to wait, but the question is, how do
we *get* to them?"

Apart from a few benches, the park to the left and
right was completely open; there was nowhere to set up
a cross fire. The matter was resolved, suddenly, horribly,
when Vladimir rose. His gun tucked in the back of his
waistband, his hands held high over his head, he began
walking toward the voices.

"*Yah galuhdyen!*" he yelled to the Germans.

There was a flurry of movement behind the fence, followed by a long, terrible silence. Then a gun was poked
through the fence.

"*Kommen!*" one of the soldiers yelled.

The boy had evidently hoped one or more of the sol-

diers would look over the pile of broken fences and concrete and make himself a target for Livingston or Ogan.
It was a brave but naive move, the lieutenant felt. Shooting at a gun might drive it back but not remove the threat.
He racked his brain for a way to attack the well-hidden
enemy.

"We can't let them take him!" Ogan said urgently.

"No," Livingston agreed, "and we can't let the enemy stay there either. Here's what I want to do. You see
where the fence is curled up and lying on its side?" Ogan
looked to where Livingston pointed. He nodded. "Whatever they drove to get here is over there. I'm going to try
to get to it."

"And do what?"

"Gun it," Livingston replied, "run them down. I'll
need you to cover me. When I start out, fire at the gun
and drive him back. As soon as you hear the vehicle start
to move, get as close to the fence as possible." He
cocked a thumb toward the flour sack at Ogan's side. "If
you have to, use a stick of dynamite to take them out."

Ogan nodded and, after taking a deep breath, Livingston sprang from behind the sandbox.

The instant he did so, Ogan opened fire and drove the
gun back. Simultaneously, Vladimir dove behind a tree,
drew his pistol, and began shooting at the fence. The
exchange lasted only a few seconds, but it was enough
time for Livingston to reach the park side of the scrap
heap. Flopping down, he took a moment to catch his
breath.

Suddenly, just a meter away, the top of the rubble was
pushed over by a German boot. Looking up, Livingston
saw a Kubel on the other side, a small Jeep-like car.
However, instead of the spare tire that these vehicles usually carried on their sloping hoods, this car boasted a
tripod-mounted MG 34 machine gun. It swung toward
Livingston, and would have cut him in half if Ogan hadn't
managed a remarkable shot, cutting down both the gun-

ner and his companion in quick succession. The gunner
fell across his weapon, pumping his only burst into the
hood of the car. The engine fell silent.

Cursing, Livingston crawled back, taking shelter behind the nearest tree. He still had no idea how many
soldiers were there, nor did it matter. Attracted by the
exchange, other soldiers came running toward the park.

Vladimir ran from one tree to another, drawing fire.
A bullet tore into his arm, but he was able to fall behind
a fat tree trunk. Having seen where two of the soldiers
were, Livingston fired several rounds, but the rubble
protected them.

Ogan looked over at Livingston, and the American
pointed to the Kubel. The machine gun seemed to be
still usable, and it was their only hope. Ogan and Vladimir both nodded, then shot at the Germans' position
to keep them back as the lieutenant bolted up and over
the woodpile.

Livingston landed on the front of the hood, at the foot
of the gun. Because the car was facing away from the
Germans, he slid down to the cobbled street. Looking
back, he saw a soldier running toward him; there was a
hollow, clumping sound as the German vaulted up the
flat back of the car and ran across the seats to take the
place of his fallen comrades. Livingston climbed to his
knees, and there was a moment when the German was
staring down the long barrel of the machine gun and
Livingston was looking up the barrel of his own pistol;
the pistol coughed first, and the soldier fell backward.

Livingston stole a look around the car. There was
only one man left of the original complement, and he
had begun making his way to the other side of the street,
away from the Kubel. The reinforcements, twenty of
them, were running toward him, double time; the surviving soldier was gesturing behind him, toward the
Jeep.

There was no time to waste. Jumping onto the hood, Livingston spun the gun around, threw the ammunition belt over his shoulder, and opened fire.

The Germans were too far from the protective doorways, too cold to think clearly, and too tired from battle. As a result, Livingston cut down most of the men on the first sweep of the gun. The survivors fell to their bellies and died reaching for their Karabiners.

Standing on top of the debris like an eagle scouting prey, Vladimir coolly shot the soldier who had tried to run. Then he ran down to check on the other soldiers.

While Ogan made certain Livingston was all right, the Russian kicked each of the soldiers. Two had survived; before Ogan or Livingston could stop him, Vladimir shot them both in the forehead.

Ogan ran over. "What the *hell* did you do that for?"

Vladimir seemed to understand. Nodding, he moved his wounded arm up and down the street. *"Da,"* he said gravely. *"Hell."*

The sergeant major said nothing more.

Noticing Vladimir's wound, Livingston insisted on taking a look at it. The bullet had only grazed the skin, and pulling his arm away, Vladimir rubbed snow on it. He insisted that he was fine.

Ogan said, "He doesn't want to miss out on the chance to do some more killing."

"You're probably right. And how do you *expect* a fourteen-year-old to react to all of this? With understanding?"

Ogan didn't answer. He looked down, sighed heavily, and walked away.

As they picked their way from doorway to doorway, Livingston realized that what made Stalingrad unique wasn't just the unusual heroism or barbarism. The entire struggle was surreal: dark gray streets, ruins, and skies splattered with blood. It was an environment in which people were reduced to something less than human, to dull, gray, killing machines.

"Hell," he said quietly.

When Masha had first mentioned the rail yards, Colon's spirits had soared.

As a child growing up in Pittsburgh, he'd often played in the rail yards. It was either that or the steelyards, and security was tighter at the mills. So he and his friends would tightrope-walk along the tracks, smoke or drink in abandoned boxcars, rumble with rich kids who had no business being there, play chicken with incoming trains, and at night, climb the power lines, set caterpillars or worms on the live wires, and bet on whose would burn the longest.

He'd felt privileged to be there then. In storybooks and in the movies, kids had to go to playgrounds, where they always did the same things, saw the same sights, played with parents looking on. But the rail yards were constantly changing, with new cars to explore and new freight to examine. And best of all, if you were careful, you never had to deal with any adults.

Now that they were at the edge of the rail yard, Colon felt his heart begin to race. He was home, and there wasn't a German soldier on the planet who could match him here. For that matter, as long as his body smarted with every step, as long as the beating he'd received was fresh in his memory, he was convinced that there wasn't a German on earth who could match him anywhere.

It was possible, though, that there was a woman who could match him. As he watched Masha go ahead with Andrei to reconnoiter, he felt certain she was the equal of any street tough, football player, or soldier he had ever met. There was an art to moving in a dangerous situation, and she knew it. She was probably as smart as any Communist could be.

She stopped behind a signal box and motioned to Colon. He and Sergei ran forward, Sergei joining Andrei behind a stack of cross-ties, Colon sliding to Masha's side.

She said, "Ahead is the bridge. This is where it becomes—how do you say it? Tricky?"

Colon looked out, saw the bridge roughly a quarter kilometer away. As they'd expected, soldiers were marching along the length of the span. Colon could also make out soldiers at either end of the trestle.

"Tricky's a good word, but from where I sit it's more like puttin' yer head in a lion's mouth. They've got a clear shot at every car in the yard. If we just run in and try to snipe at them, we're cat food."

Masha's voice hardened. "You say nothing all day, yet now you complain that it's too dangerous—"

"I *ain't* complainin'! I'm just sayin' that if we run in to draw their fire from the lieutenant, we won't be comin' out."

"You have a better idea?"

"Matter of fact, I do." Colon absently tapped his ear with his pistol. "It seems to me the thing t'do is warm the Hun slugs."

"Pardon?"

"Light a fire. Get their attention somewhere else, so that when we start shootin', they'll really have their hands full." Colon pulled matches from his pocket. "Take it from me, Masha. In the right place, a little heat can work wonders on a pack o' worms."

Masha considered this, then waved the other two Russians over and interpreted as Colon explained his strategy.

The last thing Lambert wanted was to do heavy labor. But, as he said to Weyers when they reached the lake and were struck by the enormity of the task, "The Germans will not turn around, no matter how nicely we ask. We'd better get to work." And so, under the light of the rising full moon, they began what Lambert described as "one of the most important landscaping jobs in military history.''

Lambert had Weyers take care of the lake. That was the least creative job. The South African was a good man, but he didn't have the soul of an artist. Creating a new shoreline was a different matter. Lambert felt that he would be better equipped to create the illusion that a portion of the lake was, in fact, solid earth. He thanked God it was dark. The enemy might not give the terrain a second thought.

Weyers went into the B-17 and came out with the pilot's seat. Turning it upside down, he used the backrest as a shovel, scooping snow from the other side of the plane—where the disturbance wouldn't be noticed—and dumping it near the shore. There Lambert smoothed it out, making it seem as though the shore came five meters farther into the lake than it did. When the snow was smooth and level, he gathered rocks and leaves and scattered them about.

That part of the job went quickly.

''That was easy,'' said Lambert. ''Now comes the hard part—creating the detour.''

Still panting from his exertions, Weyers muttered a string of oaths damning ''the easy part'' as he followed his partner into the woods.

One large tree had snapped nearly in two during the storm, and it was relatively simple to twist it from its trunk and drag it to the lake. But there were no other trees, and there was still a stretch of some seven meters to cover—seven meters of real shoreline before the false one.

Lambert checked the time. He began to grow anxious as Weyers tried to push down smaller trees and was unable break them. The Frenchman wasn't even sure that little trees would do the job. The plan wouldn't work if the trucks didn't leave the real shore and go onto the lake. If they used small trees, the trucks would roll right over them.

Then it hit him.

With deep sorrow, followed by a touch of nausea, Lambert went to where the two men from the B-17 were buried.

"You're not," the South African said.

"I am," Lambert replied, and began removing the rocks from the graves.

"This is sick, mate. *Very* sick."

"I know. But can you think of an alternative?"

After hesitating, Weyers said softly, "No. And I've got to believe they'd have understood. In a strange way, I guess they might even have been honored."

Bending, he scooped up an armful of stones and followed Lambert to the unblockaded stretch of shore.

Chapter Fourteen

The cap of the gas tank was frozen shut. By the time Livingston and Ogan managed to work it off, their hands were torn and bleeding; they poured in the contents of the container, and only hoped it was enough to get to the bridge.

Despite the cold, the tank started without much difficulty. It was a large, green Panzer III, and all three were able to fit inside comfortably. Because the cannon had been destroyed, and the ammunition had been taken from the hull machine guns, there was sufficient room for everyone; there was also nothing for Ogan and Vladimir to do but sit while Livingston drove. His face pressed close to the observation window, Livingston backed the tank down to level ground and guided it along the riverbank.

As they rode toward the city, Ogan found a letter tucked folded into the pistol port in the side of the turret. He held it up to the fading light by the porthole, and began to read.

"It looks like the Germans are in worse shape than we imagined." Yelling to be heard above the grinding of the gears, he said, "Listen to this. 'Dearest Father and Mother: Nothing has changed since my last letter to you. Night after night, we sit in our tents, listening to the aircraft engines and trying to guess what supplies they will bring us. Last night we got black pepper and prophylactics, but no food. We are short of all supplies. Each man is given a hundred grams of bread, and watery soup, which we try to improve by stirring it with bones from horses that we dig up. Some of the soldiers actually get to kill and eat horses, but my division, being motorized, is not included in this plan. We are also low on firewood, and because petrol is so difficult to come by, we can make only limited trips into the city to fetch kindling. Ironically, the Russian pigs are able to stay warm at night by burning the ruins of their own buildings. In the morning, when they are fresh, we are frozen.' ''

Livingston said, ''I don't hurt for them.''

''Wait, there's more. 'Though we continue to fight, there is word that Russian reinforcements are on the way: Rokossovsky from the north, and Vatutin from the west. If this is so, then the sad truth is that we have not yet seen the worst of this war.' ''

Livingston's ears perked. ''So that's it, then. The reason for this mustard-gas operation. They don't want to have to fight the armies as well as snipers in the city.''

''So it would seem. But why do you suppose Escott and Sweet didn't tell us that reinforcements are coming?''

''Probably because they're top secret. That's why only the Germans know.''

The tank rocked and lurched up the dirt road, past the tunnel where Leonid had been captured, then pressed on into the city.

The streets were virtually deserted now, all German personnel having been diverted—probably to guard the shipments. Livingston began to dread what they'd find at the terminal, though he took some consolation from the fact that at least he'd sent Colon ahead. By the time they arrived, there might not be a railroad, let alone any Germans.

Things would have been easier if it hadn't snowed. The wooden cars were damp and the cross-ties were covered with lumpy sheets of ice. Still, Colon felt that the plan would work.

Though the fuel had probably been drained from the cranes and other machines in the service area, kerosene lamps were still hanging from several of the cars. The Russians covered Colon as he moved around and under the trains, draining the lanterns into a rusty bucket he'd found.

When Colon returned, he told the others that he wanted to try to get to the service area in the middle of the yard.

"You're mad!" Masha said. "What's wrong with the cars here?"

"They're too wet. Look." He pointed ahead. "There are three cars coupled at the service platform, under a ledge. They'll be drier, an' if I can get them to burn, the wooden building'll go up too."

"But how will you *get* there?"

Colon studied the terrain. "Whatta we got? Three . . . four freight cars side by side, an open stretch of track, then a turntable, more open track, and then the service area."

"After the freight cars, you'd be out in the open."

"Not me. You guys."

"What?"

"Yeah, an' the open space won't matter, because the Heinies'll be lookin' somewhere else."

Masha shook her head. "I'm sorry, but I don't understand."

Before answering, Colon studied the terminal. It was on the other side of the yard from the service area. Out-

side the main building were two water tanks and a tower
that contained sand for use on icy tracks.

"Look," he said, "we do *two* diversions. Those supports on the sand tower look like they're as old as my
grandmother. The thing'll burn like dry leaves."

"So? Once the fire reaches the water towers, it will
be extinguished."

"By then, it won't matter. When the legs start to burn,
you three run in the other direction, toward the service
area, and torch the trains there. We'll have a fire in the
north, a fire in the south, and the jerks won't know which
way to turn. Meanwhile, we all meet back here and start
a fire from the west. They'll think they've got the whole
Russian army comin' down their throats."

Masha considered the plan. "There are problems. How
will you take the kerosene over?"

"You can thank your countrymen for that." Colon disappeared into the boxcar and returned with an empty
vodka bottle. "I noticed it before. I'll use it to make
myself a little cocktail."

"And there's something else. By setting this fire before Livingston arrives, you will alert the enemy that
there are saboteurs among them. Is that wise?"

Colon gestured toward the bridge. "Hell, they're expectin' us already. Besides"—he glanced at his watch—
"it's less than fifteen minutes before the lieutenant
arrives. It's about time we started making things hot for
these Kraut bastards."

Masha consulted the others, and they agreed to the
plan. After mapping a route that would take him under
as many cars as possible, and then waiting until the sun
had slid behind the terminal, Colon filled the bottle and
set out.

The sound arrived long before the trucks themselves.
Tucked behind a thick clump of saplings, Weyers and
Lambert had been watching the dark lake. When Lam-

bert wasn't studying the shore, wondering if there were
any last-minute touch-ups he should make, he stared at
the B-17. The wind obscured the plane with clouds of
snow; the hazy image reminded Lambert of a mirage.

But the graves were real. The stiff, obscenely slashed
bodies of the pilot and copilot were real. His hate, too,
was real.

He was glad to finally hear the rumbling. It meant that
there was no more time to second-guess their handiwork,
to worry whether or not it would fool the Germans. Now,
it was all in the laps of the gods.

The grinding of the treads was accented, now and then,
by the snap of branches, the thud of trees. The distant
glow of the lanterns through the trees was like fireflies.

"God help us if they're just running everything
down," Weyers said.

Lambert hadn't needed to hear that. "God help us is
right. If the barrier doesn't work, we have only one re-
course left."

"And what's that?"

Lambert muttered, "Snowballs."

Soon the men could hear the crunch of the soldiers'
boots. They huddled lower behind the trees.

The first truck surged into the clearing like a lion
bounding from its lair. It shot over a ridge of snow and
slammed down on the ground, the treads kicking up twin
plumes of snow. The second truck leapt into the clearing
some twenty meters beyond, the two lines of soldiers
marching alongside them both. Under the bright moonlight, the men could also see the trucks' vile cargo quite
clearly: two huge, cylindrical yellow tanks boldly marked
GIFTGAS. Poison gas.

After the trucks emerged in the clearing, Lambert began to worry that the second truck was too far behind
the first. If one sunk right away, there would be enough
time for the other to stop.

Too late to worry, he told himself. There was nothing to do now but sit and watch.

The driver of the lead truck turned to avoid the tree they'd put down, and Lambert's spirits rose. The truck swung toward the lake, then slowed as he approached the graves. The driver peered out the side window, shouted to a major, a chemical warfare officer, walking beside the truck.

"Herr Regierungschemiker—do you think these are ours?"

"Nein."

Lambert's heart was thudding against his throat as the driver shifted gears. *"Mon Dieu*, please, *please*—"

"Wait!" the officer shouted, cupping a hand to his mouth. "Don't run them down. The rocks may be *frozen.* They'll rip the bottom of the truck! Go *around* the graves!"

Acknowledging with a wave, the driver shifted gears and turned the truck toward the lake.

Lambert watched, cursing as the windswept clouds and the snow billowing from beneath the treads obscured his view. The first truck was no longer visible, and he felt a surge of hope as the second truck disappeared into its wake. But that hope died as, like a monster from the depths, the first truck reappeared, rolling up from the lake and back toward the shore.

"The bloody ice is holding!" Weyers snarled. "How is that possible?"

"I don't know—"

Weyers jumped to his feet. "Hell, they're not getting away. I'm gonna go and jump on the goddamn lake my—"

The rest of his exclamation was drowned out by a deep, resounding pop from deep within the white cloud of snow over the lake. It was followed by the sounds of splashing water.

Now Lambert rose. "The second truck must have gone under!"

Both men watched through the trees as the driver of the first truck stopped, jumped out, and ran toward the lake. Now that the treads were still, the Frenchman could see what had happened. The front end of the Maultier was jutting straight from the water. All around it, soldiers were helping their fellows from the lake.

Lambert shook his head angrily, like a dog with a bone. "I won't let one truck get through."

"What are you going to do?"

"Just stay here," the Frenchman said, and ran from the woods.

The South African raised his gun, watching as Lambert forged through the snow. The Germans were too busy pulling each other from the water to notice another man in a German uniform. If they had, Weyers was ready to buy him every possible second.

Lambert covered the fifty meters to the truck, then ducked inside. Throwing the truck into reverse, he waited until it began edging backward, then flung himself out the door.

There were shouts as men saw the truck coming toward them, and oaths as it picked up speed. The huge Opel hit the lake with a thump, then stalled. It sat there for a moment, and then, as though a trapdoor had opened beneath it, the truck plunged through the ice. The surface of the lake rippled and cracked, men shouting and vanishing as the frigid waters swallowed them. The turbulence sent the other truck over onto its back, trapping the tank of mustard gas beneath it. Steam rose from the engines of the two trucks, large bubbles bursting where they sank.

A few men who had stayed on the shore shot at Lambert, but Weyers's return fire sent them retreating to the far side of the lake, where they took cover behind a string of boulders. Picking himself up, the Frenchman ran for the clump of trees.

"That was good," Weyers said as he continued to shoot at the Germans, "but why didn't you *take* the damn truck? We could have dumped the gas somewhere, and then we wouldn't have had to walk back to Stalingrad."

Lambert drew his own pistol and fired several rounds. "I wanted the gas *gone, mon ami*. I did get this, though." He pulled a crumpled map from his coat. "It was lying on the seat. At least we'll be able to find the most direct route back to the city."

Weyers and Lambert picked off several soldiers who managed to pull themselves from the water. Then, still firing, they began their retreat.

Exhausted as they were, the Frenchman couldn't help but smile. "You know what's most amazing, Wings? That we actually managed to follow our original orders."

"How's that?"

"What was our mission?"

"To sink the gas."

"And what did we do?"

Weyers frowned as they stopped firing and began to run through the woods. "Look at it a different way, Rotter."

"Ah, the voice of the pragmatist."

"Call me names if ya want, but tell me who *really* sunk the Jerries—us or the B-17 crew?"

Lambert's smile evaporated. "*C'est vrai*. It *is* they who deserve the medals."

Only the howling of the wind, the lengthening shadows of late afternoon, and their thoughts of the brave fliers accompanied the men as they made their way in silence through the woods.

The tank lumbered past a row of ramshackle log huts on the outskirts of the train yard. It was nearly five, and the sun was down. There was less than two hours before the train reached the terminal.

The railroad workers once lived at this end, men whose lives were directed by the howl of incoming trains. The trains would call and, regardless of the hour, the men would go out and pamper them.

Ironically, Livingston thought, these men and their kind understood discomfort and sacrifice. Unwittingly, in modernizing the railroads, Stalin had prepared his people for the deprivation that was to follow.

After passing the nine shacks, and the huge iron and rubber bumpers that marked the end of the rail line, Livingston maneuvered the tank onto the tracks.

Ahead, roughly an eighth of a kilometer away, was the bridge. Soldiers stood shoulder to shoulder along its entire length, and also as far as he could see on either side.

The tracks slipped by. Now and then, a soldier would look back at them, then turn away. Because he was driving a German tank, no one gave him a second thought.

Vladimir hugged the dynamite to him. Ogan had managed to explain the plan, telling the boy that they'd park the tank beneath the bridge, light the fuses, then evacuate. But Vladimir shook his head, said that he didn't want to run the risk of the tank's containing the blast. He wanted to make sure the bridge came down. And the only way to do that was for him to get out and slap the explosives beneath the trestle.

The plan was extremely dangerous, from Vladimir's point of view. But neither of them could deny that it would be more effective. Nor could they have talked the Russian out of it if they'd wanted to. Indeed, as they neared the bridge, Vladimir seemed almost buoyant, eager for the chance to strike back at the enemy.

When they were just two hundred meters away, Ogan pushed at the hatch. There was a moment of concern when it refused to budge, but it gave when Ogan and the youth both put their shoulders to it.

Ogan went to the pistol port, did his best to draw a bead on the bridge. The clank of the hatch drew some attention, and soldiers who turned now continued to look down at the tank.

"We've got them asking questions," Ogan warned.

Livingston handed Vladimir the matches. "Good. Because it's time to give them some answers."

Livingston and the Russian shared a long, respectful look, after which Vladimir lit the dynamite. The fuses cast a bright, blinding light through the tank, and Livingston had to shield his eyes to see the terrain ahead. An *oberst* had been summoned, and was leaning imperiously on the railing, shouting down. Several soldiers, rifles held across their chests, stood at his side.

Livingston said, "He wants us to identify ourselves, Ken."

"If you can swing me to the side just a bit, I'll be happy to oblige."

Livingston turned the wheel slightly, and the tank moved ahead diagonally. The maneuver gave Ogan a clear view of the bridge, and though the tank was rocking vigorously, he managed to spray the target area with gunfire. Livingston was pleased that though Ogan was a professional bleeding heart, he also knew when to stanch the flow.

The railing stopped most of the bullets, but a soldier and the *oberst* went down.

"Good job," Livingston said.

Livingston straightened their course, but when the tank was just a few meters from the bridge, he swung diagonally again.

"Give them another round, Ken. I don't want them shooting down the hatch."

Ogan slapped in his last clip and fired slowly at the bridge. Two more soldiers fell, and a few Karabiners poked through the rails, one shot blazing through the observation window, right past Livingston's cheek. But then they were under the bridge and Vladimir hopped up through the canopy.

"Good luck!" Livingston shouted as the boy climbed onto the turret, the dynamite blazing in a bundle under one arm.

Livingston stopped the tank and watched through the observation port as the boy looked for a place to lay the sticks. He tried to wedge it in a V-shaped joint between two of the girders, but the metal was too thin and the bundle wouldn't balance there.

Livingston licked his lips as the fuses shrank. There were shouts from above, and the clatter of boots. Soldiers were running from the bridge toward the wall that bordered the lower tracks.

They were coming down.

Aware of the soldiers, Vladimir rattled a fist in frustration. He squinted into the darkness above, studied a platform where the shoe connected the middle support to the span. He looked back at Livingston and, with a smile, used his foot to slam the hatch shut.

"Vladimir! What the hell are you doing?"

"He's climbing, sir! He's going up the support!"

"They'll cut him in half!" With a snarl, Livingston threw the tank into reverse. "Ken, can you cover him?"

Ogan was already looking out the port, and began shooting at the soldiers as they tried to come down the wall onto the lower tracks. Suddenly, the healthy shout of the pistol was replaced by a soft click.

"Empty," Ogan said with disgust.

Livingston continued to back up, watching as Vladimir scaled the girders. He lay the dynamite on the small square of metal. Swearing, Livingston threw the tank ahead.

"Ken, get ready to open the—"

The roar followed the blaze by a heartbeat. It hadn't come from the bridge but from the terminal, from a rickety wooden tower.

"Must be Colon!" Ogan shouted.

Livingston nodded as he pressed the controls, trying to get every available ounce of speed from the tank. He looked out as Vladimir just clung there in the shadows, his grim expression illuminated by the flickering fuse.

"Hold on, kid, just hold on!"

Suddenly the world went white, as the bridge, the soldiers, and part of the terminal flew in pieces into the air.

Chapter Fifteen

Blinded by the blast, Livingston plowed into the wall. Several soldiers fell as the stone edifice crumbled; Ogan and Livingston themselves were thrown back as the tank came to rest at a sharp angle. Grabbing the controls, the lieutenant pulled himself up, spitting out dust and particles of stone that had been blown through the observation window. There were shouts and gunfire all around them, followed by a hard rapping on the hatch of the tank.

"Lieutenant! Are you okay? *Lieutenant!*"

Reaching up, Livingston threw back the hatch. A Karabiner was thrust into his hand.

"Here's one for the sergeant major too," Colon said, handing down another rifle.

"The bridge?" Livingston said.

"Ain't nothing there 'cept air." He smiled. Spinning, he sprayed gunfire behind him, then looked back into the hatch. "Come on, sir. We can't let Masha and her pals fight this thing on their own."

Livingston accepted Colon's hand and climbed through the hatch.

The rail yard was an inferno, flames rising from the cars, repair platform, and terminal, an inferno peppered with white flashes as fuel or ammunition exploded.

"It was somethin'!" Colon enthused. "The sand tower fell right away, set off fuel or explosives or whatever the hell they had in the terminal. Took a pisspot fulla Krauts with it."

Livingston commended him and, as he helped the dazed Ogan from the tank, he scanned the wreckage of the bridge. There were bodies and parts of bodies lying amid the rubble. He didn't see a trace of Vladimir but knew there was no way he could have survived.

Through the smoke of the smoldering bridge, Livingston could see Masha and her people advancing across the tracks. "Come on," he said, "we've still got a train to catch."

While Ogan and Colon set up covering fire, Livingston climbed from the tank, ran across the tracks, and stepping over a pile of bodies, scaled the wall on the opposite side of the track. Colon went next, grabbing a second Karabiner as he ran, and, holding both waist high, fired from the hip at anything that had a uniform and wasn't dead. When Livingston and Colon had taken up positions on the far side, Ogan scurried across the tracks.

By this time, reinforcements were pouring from the terminal. Livingston guessed there were at least one hundred soldiers converging on the rail yard, most of them stepping over the wounded and the dead, taking up positions behind smoking rubble or still-flaming trains.

Livingston said, "We'll have to hurry. As soon as they realize there's only a handful of us, they'll charge us."

"Then we can't let 'em realize that," Colon replied, firing across the tracks.

Masha and Sergei came running past the destroyed bridge. They dropped flat beside Livingston.

"Fine job," he said, then frowned. "Where's Andrei?"

"He had an idea." She pointed to a smoking locomotive and freight train that had begun inching toward them from well down the track.

"With all the smoke and fire around, no one saw him stoke it. He felt it would give us extra cover."

"Good idea," Livingston said as the old, black locomotive chugged toward them. "I suggest we take advantage of it."

Everyone but Colon turned and started toward the north.

"Private! Let's move it out!"

"You go, sir! Someone's got to cover for Andrei!"

Colon lay there and watched as the burning train headed toward the wreck of the bridge. Soldiers retreated as the fiery train picked up speed, most of them diving to their bellies as the locomotive hit the twisted girders with a grating smack. It threw them in all directions, the impact also derailing the train. The locomotive skidded off the terminal side of the track bed, dust and stone flying as it plowed into the shattered wall below. The other cars slammed into the engine and folded one into the other, throwing slats of wood and burning embers in all directions.

Glancing down the track, Colon saw Andrei approaching from behind the wreckage. He was covered with blood and dragging a leg.

Leaving one of his guns behind, Colon ran toward the tracks. Before he'd taken more than a few steps, however, a burst of gunfire brought Andrei down.

"No!" Colon stopped, aimed, and shot at a German soldier who was lying behind an overturned truck. A German helmet ducked back and Colon continued toward Andrei.

Watching from the other side of the tracks, Livingston and Masha set up a protective fire as Colon knelt beside the Russian. He put his ear to Andrei's chest, felt his wrist. Screaming, he ran across the tracks, toward the German side.

"Colon!" Livingston hollered.

The private either ignored him or didn't hear him.

Oblivious to his own pain, the deep wounds from the beating, Colon ran around the flaming train and up the shattered wall to the overturned truck. The German's rifle came around the fender, but Colon swung his own Karabiner, using it like a club, to smack the other gun away. Then he flipped the rifle around, aimed, and fired twice. He looked down for a moment; satisfied, he turned and ran back across the track, scooping up an armful of rifles as he crossed.

"That was a damn foolish thing to do," Livingston said when Colon rejoined them.

"I know, sir, but Andrei bought us time. His killer *needed* to die."

There was no disputing Colon's logic and, after making sure that Masha and Sergei were all right, Livingston distributed the extra guns, then led the team into the field beyond the tracks. Despite what had just happened, the Russian woman's face was as impassive as ever. He couldn't help but wonder if it would remain so when, at last, they came face-to-face with the cargo that had cost her so dearly.

The team proceeded in leapfrog fashion. Two of them stayed behind at all times to cover their backs. When the other four had gone approximately one hundred meters, two of them would peel off and the other two would catch up.

They'd gone just over a kilometer when they saw the train.

It was coming out of the large, low moon, and looked like something a child might have designed using toy soldiers—overcrowded and overarmed. There were soldiers riding on the locomotive, standing on the injector pipe, holding on to the handrail, and hanging on to the window. There were also men on the flatbed car, surrounding the two gas tanks, and there were rifles pointing from the ports of the armored car and caboose. There were even soldiers standing on the couplers and on the front of the locomotive.

"Looks like they're expectin' company," Colon said.

Livingston agreed. The Germans were indeed prepared for a massive assault, and the lieutenant bitterly regretted that he wouldn't be able to give it to them.

Livingston looked around. The track passed through a plain that sloped gently toward them, to the west. There was a barren, snow-covered field to the north of the tracks; to the south, several broken carts and a rusted plow. Beyond the implements was a ramshackle shed and more acres of white terrain. The burned skeleton of a barn was well in the distance.

In just a moment, the men in the train would spot them. Livingston ordered the team behind the sled. After surveying the field one last time, he joined them.

"The way I see it, we've got to concentrate on the locomotive. If we can take it and run the train backwards, fine. Failing that, let's at least try to uncouple it. If we have to, we'll start shooting holes in the gas tanks, release the stuff here. With any luck, it won't drift far."

The ground began to tremble as the train neared.

"You're gonna want someone shootin' from the other side," Colon said. "I'll go."

"No. We attack from this side. At least we've got cover. We'll go after the men on this side of the locomotive, and whoever's in the cab. We'll worry about the other side when we get on board."

As they crouched beside the shack, Ogan sidled up to Livingston. "For what it's worth, sir, I think you've done a hell of a job getting us this far."

"It was all of us," Livingston said, glancing over at the Russians. "Everyone did their job."

Masha was watching the tracks from around the corner of the shed. "They're slowing!"

"Someone must have radioed ahead," Ogan said, "or maybe they saw the smoke from the terminal."

"They're stopping," Masha said. After a moment, she added, "That's strange."

"What is?"

"Before, they were pulling an engine in back. Now they are not."

"Freight trains usually travel wit' a spare," said Colon. "They must've dumped it to conserve—"

"Soldiers are coming from the armored car and flatbed," Masha interrupted. "They're walking along tracks."

"They *must* have gotten word about us," Ogan said.

"I vote we attack," Colon added. "If they pin us here, this isn't gonna be a happy fight."

Livingston looked around. Colon had a point, but he didn't relish attacking more than three dozen soldiers. The rotted carts offered no defense, and going inside the shack would be suicidal. He pursed his lips and wormed over to Masha's side.

"I'd give my right arm for a hand grenade," he said as the Germans fanned out, obviously intending to surround the place. "I don't like the odds, Masha, but it looks as though Colon's right. We're going to have to take the offensive, and hope that one of us gets close enough to the tanks to put a few holes in them."

"Agreed," she said.

"We'll let them get a little farther from the train, so they can't use it for cover."

Colon said, "Wouldn't it be a kick in the head if we go ahead and get killed—and Rotter and Wings failed?"

"A riot," Ogan said. He gripped his rifle tightly and forced a smile. "But Rotter didn't fail, God bless him. He and Wings probably sunk the ships and then went looking for a sunlamp."

"Or a dame."

"Or a train!" Livingston said. "I'll be goddamned, will you look at this?"

The others rolled out slightly so they could see. The

Germans also stopped and turned, watched as a lone locomotive rocketed along the tracks. Lambert was leaning
from the window, illuminated by the steady fire from his
MP38, which he was directing at the soldiers on the
tracks. An *oberst* standing in the cab screamed for the
soldiers to board.

Masha said, "That was the spare locomotive."

"He's got one hell of a head of steam," Ogan said.
"He's going to ram them."

"Let's give them something to think about on this
side," Livingston said.

Diving sideways, clear of all obstacles, Colon began
shooting. Before the Germans had turned back to face
the attack, his bullets killed five of them. The two Russians went around the shack, firing as they ran toward
the train, while Ogan and Livingston covered them from
behind the shack. Half the Germans who had left the
train were dead before the others could organize to meet
both fronts.

On the locomotive, the *oberst* pushed at his engineer,
and the train began to move again.

"We can't let him through," Livingston said. "Go
after the damn locomotive!"

He came from behind the shed and, following Colon,
ran down the other side of the tracks. Ogan ran after
Masha and, from the corner of his eye, Livingston saw
the Russian woman spin and go down. Sergei looked
back; Ogan waved him on as he slid to her side.

"Go ahead," she said, clutching her thigh. "I'm all
right."

"Are you sure?"

"Yes! *Get the train.*"

The ground was quickly staining red beneath her.
"We'll be back for you," the Englishman said, and hurried forward.

Livingston was still firing, still waiting for the train to
pass, when plumes of red began spraying from the backs

and legs of the Germans the *oberst* had left behind. Lambert had come within range, and was stitching the few men who survived with bursts from his pistol. Clearly, all that mattered to the *oberst* now was outrunning Weyers's locomotive.

Ahead of Livingston, a bullet from the German train knocked Colon onto his back. A stream of gunfire also forced Livingston, Ogan, and Sergei to seek cover on their respective sides of the track. As the train roared by, the few guns still active in the caboose kept them pinned where they were.

When the train had passed, Livingston rose.

"Damn! *Damn!*"

He glanced ahead at Colon, who waved weakly. Then he looked at Weyers's engine, which was racing toward him. Throwing his rifle over his back and jamming his pistol in the pocket of his Russian coat, he ran toward the track.

"No!" the South African yelled. "Don't try it!"

"Like hell I won't," Livingston said under his breath. As the locomotive passed, the lieutenant reached out and grabbed the ladder behind the coal tender. The maneuver nearly dislocated both arms, but he held on. Locking his feet around the rung, he got a better grip and then pulled himself up into the coal bin. Hurrying across the scraps of coal that remained, he climbed into the cab.

"That was *tres* impressive, sir," Lambert said, "but I'm afraid you will never play the piano again."

Livingston rubbed his right shoulder. The warmth from the open coal furnace felt good. "What the hell are you two doing here?"

"Seeing the countryside, sir."

Livingston frowned. "The gas—"

"We took care of it, lieutenant. As for being here, we located the tracks thanks to a map we took from the Germans. We thought it would be the best way to meet up with the rest of you. We rode a hand cart until we discovered this locomotive a few kilometers back." He cocked a thumb toward a transmitter in the control panel. "We were not far away when we heard someone from the terminal radio ahead about a fire. It didn't take a genius to figure out the rest."

"You saved our skins," Livingston said as he looked ahead at the German train. "What are you planning to do now?"

Weyers said without turning, "We're going to stop them, sir."

"That's fine, but you can't derail them. This close to the terminal, they can still get the gas into Stalingrad."

Weyers moved the throttle and they gained slightly on the train. "I have no intention of derailing them, sir. This is a Gelsky train, sir. We've got a coupler in front. Rotter," he yelled over his shoulder, "I'm gonna need more fire! I'm really pushing her now."

Sighing, Lambert grabbed a shovel and began feeding coal into the open furnace. Livingston helped by picking up chunks and throwing them in.

Soldiers in the caboose began firing at them as the locomotive gained on them. The engine clanged as bullets struck inside and out; Livingston and Colon bent, but Weyers continued to stare ahead. He didn't flinch even when the window exploded and showered him with glass.

"All right," he said when just a few meters separated the two trains, "I'm going to make my move!"

Livingston stood and watched as they closed, slowly, on the caboose. And he realized, then, that Weyers had no intention of hitting the train at all.

The lunatic was going to try to grab it.

Chapter Sixteen

Weyers was literally nursing the throttle as he approached, edging the stick forward, then back. He was no longer gaining in meters but in centimeters, the caboose within arm's length, the couplers brushing.

The South African gave the locomotive a jolt and the couplers connected. The instant he heard the distinctive clack of the latch, Weyers yelled for the men to brace themselves, then pulled on the air brakes.

Though prepared, the three men were hurled against the control panel. The locomotive squealed violently and, climbing back to his feet, Livingston could see sparks flying across the snow; the smell of ozone filled his nostrils.

The locked trains ground to a halt. Looking ahead, Livingston could see the ruined bridge and flaming terminal.

"Tug-o'-war time," Weyers said, and threw the locomotive into reverse. The wheels screamed and pistons howled as the engine began creeping backward. "Give me more fire, Rotter!"

Lambert and Livingston began tossing more coal into the furnace. Over the din, the lieutenant could barely make out the *oberst* screaming at his men.

"What's he barking about?" Lambert asked.

Livingston stopped shoveling and listened.

"What is it, sir? Can you make it out?"

Swearing, Livingston grabbed his rifle and scampered up the control panel to the shattered windshield. He paused and said, "Cover me, Rotter. The sonofabitch is going to uncouple the trains."

Squeezing through, the lieutenant leapt over the steam dome and sidestepped the whistle. Lying down behind the smokestack, he hooked his feet through the handrails that ran along the top of the locomotive.

The locomotive was higher than the caboose and the armored car, and he had a relatively clear shot at both. The few soldiers left in the caboose were trying to make their way forward; after Livingston picked the first two off, the others retreated. Return fire from the armored car flew wide of Livingston's position, the portholes having been designed to cover only the sides of the train. The smokestack rendered the 76.2mm gun on top useless. Leaning from the cabin, Lambert drove back the few soldiers who came out to try to get a clear shot.

Weyers's engine began to pick up speed, and the entire train started rolling backward.

"Just as I figured!" Weyers cheered. "The bugger's all but run out of coal!"

Suddenly, the train lurched to a stop again as the engineer on the German train applied his own brakes. As soon as it did so, a handful of men came from the locomotive, pale, surreal figures in the stark moonlight. Two of them set up a cross fire on the smokestack, while a third and fourth made their way onto the flatbed. Before ducking to safety, Livingston saw that they had chain cutters.

There were two massive chains holding the gas tanks side by side on the flatbed. One was draped across the front, one across the back. The *oberst* intended to unload the gas here, and probably try to haul it into the city.

"Lieutenant!" Weyers yelled. "He got us that time. It'll be a few minutes before I've got the *oomph* to override him!"

"We don't *have* a few minutes!" Livingston yelled. "They're dumping the gas tanks!"

"Like hell they are!" Lambert yelled, bolting from the cab door like a human cannonball. "Not after all we've been through!"

The Frenchman followed a spray of gunfire as he ran along the side of the train. Gunfire from inside the armored car, however, sent the Frenchman jumping back against the side of the locomotive.

"Maybe some other time, *oui*?"

"Stay put," Livingston said. "Just keep an eye on the back of the flatbed—don't let them uncouple it!"

Save for the coughing of the locomotive, there was silence as the Germans worked on the chains at the back of the flatbed. The armored car obstructed his view completely, and rushing them would be suicidal; he could do nothing until the soldiers went to release the chains in front.

As he lay there, the cars once again began to ease backward under the pull of Weyers's engine. The German locomotive complained, but it wasn't able to hold its ground. Black clouds rose around him, and the heat of the engine roof began to burn his coat. He knew he wouldn't be able to stay there for long.

Lambert walked backward, alongside the train. He stayed wide enough to keep an eye on the coupler between the flatbed and the armored car; the gas tanks prevented the Germans from having a clear shot at him.

As they began to pick up speed, Livingston saw movement below, on the western side. Inching over, he saw three soldiers using the shadow of the train to try to reach the caboose and uncouple it. Livingston shot down at them, and the men ducked between the cars. Shifting quickly to the other side, the lieutenant got Lambert's attention. He held up three fingers and pointed to the coupler; nodding, the Frenchman stopped walking. As the coupler section passed, he shot the men dead.

The locomotive screeched and slowed again. Smoke poured from the German locomotive as the engineer obviously stoked his engine with everything he had left. It was then, over the din of the engines, that Livingston heard the order he'd been dreading: With a steady wind blowing in from the north, the *oberst* told the men on the flatbed to release the gas.

The valves were in the back, where the men already were. There was no way Livingston could stop them from atop the locomotive: He'd have to go forward.

"Lambert! Up here!"

Even before the Frenchman had climbed the ladder, Livingston had gone to the front of the locomotive, swung down to the headlight in the center of the boiler front, and jumped onto the back of the iron-plated caboose. Reaching up with his pistol, he fired into one of the ports, then ran up the ladder in back to the top of the car. Gunfire cracked from behind him as Lambert kept the soldiers in the armored car from opening the rear door. Just then, Livingston heard a yell from behind as a sudden down draft swept the dark cloud from the smokestack into Lambert's face. Livingston turned just in time to see the Frenchman's rifle slip from his hands as he reflexively pressed them to his eyes.

Livingston had no choice but to continue, and scurrying along on his belly, he reached the end of the caboose, crouched, and jumped to the armored boxcar.

Weyers's engine was beginning to win the battle again, and under the strident cries of the *oberst*, Livingston could hear the soldiers working frantically to open the tanks. As the train had passed earlier, Livingston had seen that the valve screws were driven by wheels twice the size of a manhole cover. It would take a few minutes to crank it open.

Livingston raced ahead. Just as he rounded the turret containing the 76.2mm guns, a soldier's head appeared at the far end of the car, along with a Luger; it cracked twice and a bullet caught Livingston in the side. He fell onto his belly and, despite the pain, managed to crawl back behind the turret.

The train was picking up speed, heading away from the city. Livingston leaned on the turret, waited for the soldier to show himself again. There was more yelling, this time from the flatbed. He wormed forward on his good side, slowly, painfully, half expecting to see smudges of gas rise above the roof of the boxcar. It hurt worse than the wound to think that they'd come this far, only to be a few bullets away from succeeding.

But instead of the gas, he heard shots from the flatbed, and then from the western side of the train. Looking over, he saw Ogan and Sergei crouched behind a snowbank, firing at the soldiers. Livingston dragged himself forward, peered over the edge of the car. The four soldiers were hiding behind the tanks, shooting back. The *oberst* came out and was firing as well.

They'd forgotten about Livingston. He'd make them wish they hadn't. Leaning on the top rung of a ladder, he rose to his knees.

"Gute nacht, meine herren!" he said and, raising his pistol, shot from the hip. They fell in turn, the *oberst* dropping to the side, between the flatbed and the locomotive.

Painfully lowering himself to the flatbed, Livingston went to check on the forward chain when the engineer came from the locomotive and began firing—not at Livingston, but at the gas tanks. Two of his bullets struck one of the tanks, and a greasy, yellow smoke began to drift from the side.

Livingston shot the engineer, then, dizzy from the loss of blood, fell beside the tank. Grabbing the chain that was still attached to the tanks, Ogan pulled himself up.

He climbed between the flatbed and the locomotive and, grabbing the lever that linked the couplers, pulled up. There was a loud snap, a surge of speed, and the German locomotive began to recede and slow.

Ogan came over. Livingston was coughing, unable to hold his breath. Putting his arm across his back, Ogan rose and was nearly knocked over by the tanks, which, held by just one chain, swayed precariously as the train picked up speed. Dropping to his knees, the Englishman crawled to the side of the flatbed and heaved Livingston over. The lieutenant landed in the snow, and Ogan followed him off.

The sergeant major landed on his shoulder and rolled through the snow. When he got his bearings, he saw Livingston lying several meters away and hurried over.

When he arrived, Livingston managed to prop himself on an elbow. Together, they watched as the train, racing now, headed back toward the fields trailing a thick column of black smoke and, below it, a thinner column of yellow poison. He lay back.

"Weyers—Lambert. Did they get off?"

"Naturellement," said the Frenchman.

The two were plodding over from the south. They'd obviously bailed out before Ogan and Livingston.

"That's what I like," Livingston said. "Men who stick with something to the end."

"There was nothing else we could do," Weyers said as he squinted through the fading light at the train.

"Besides, Lieutenant," said Lambert, "we did our job. We assumed that you were capable of doing yours."

Livingston managed a weak smile and lay back. He looked up at Weyers, who was towering above him. There were dark circles around his eyes and grime on his cheeks and forehead, his face was drawn, and he was panting heavily. But Livingston couldn't remember when he'd seen a more satisfied smile on anyone's lips.

Sergei joined the group.

"The others," Livingston said. "How are they?"

Ogan told him about Masha, then asked Sergei about Colon. The Russian pointed to his left shoulder. "Colon—*mnyeh zdyes balna.*"

"Shot in the shoulder," Ogan said.

Lambert said, "Between that and the prison, there is one man who will be sore come morning."

Just then, there was a grating sound from well up the tracks. The men watched as, in the distance, the runaway train hopped the track, dragging its deadly cargo with it. The furnace exploded and, amid the billowing black smoke, the yellow fumes twined slowly, wraithlike, from the wreckage. It hung low over the wreckage; only the fringes of the cloud were disturbed by the wind.

"It'll dissipate slowly," Ogan said, "but I doubt that it will get anywhere near the city."

Lambert shook his head. "All this, an' a train wreck too. *Mes amis*—it's almost like *Noel!*"

Weyers and Ogan helped Livingston back to the shed, where they were joined by Colon and Lambert. The men lay Livingston down beside Masha and, after bandaging his wound with fur torn from the pockets of their coats, they went outside and began forming the boards of the cart into a sledge.

Though they didn't think the Germans would come after them in the dark and subzero temperatures, they had to leave. The gas cloud was creeping toward them. Under the full moon, the low-lying poison almost seemed to glow as it rolled along, a meter above the ground.

"I've seen mustard gas before," said Weyers as he lay Livingston on the stripped-down cart, "but whatever the Nazis did to make it cling like that is vile."

"I wish we could take back a sample," Ogan said. "Maybe there's a way to counteract the stuff."

"We've *got* the way," replied the South African. "It's

called *leaving.*'' He looked across the field again, shuddered like a child. ''And the sooner, the better.''

Their destination was a car factory less than a quarter of a mile from the Volga. The Russians had converted it to a tank factory, and the Germans had burned it; however, because it was so far northeast of the city, neither the Russians nor the Germans had bothered basing people there. Nevertheless, as a place for exhausted refugees to spend the night, it was ideal.

The snow had melted slightly during the day, and it had frozen again when the sun went down, giving the team a hard, slick surface for the sledge. Though the trek was demanding, and the temperatures bitter, there was no wind, and they completed the trip by dawn. Livingston couldn't believe it had been just two days, exactly, since they'd arrived in Russia. But again, as in Algiers, despite everything that had happened—or *because* of it?— they had been two of the most rewarding days of his life.

After settling in amid the charred machines of the cavernous factory, they fed on hares Weyers and Sergei had shot. At the express request of the South African, Lambert was barred from participating in the hunt.

After resting for a full day, the group headed for the Volga. The sight that greeted them caused them to stop in their tracks.

A wave of Russian infantry was moving in from the north: on gunboats, down the shores, through the fields, and along the bluffs. In the distance, the commandos could vaguely make out T-70 light tanks, and the heavier T-34s; trucks carrying rocket-launchers and stacks of 132mm rockets; and rows of sleek 45mm field guns. On the other side of the river, the armies that had been holding the line there were now advancing southwest, toward the German batteries that guarded the river.

''Holy Moses,'' Weyers muttered, his exclamation speaking for his teammates, who stood in awed silence. Masha and Sergei broke down and cried.

The group was spotted by a young lieutenant at the front of the lines, who ran ahead with five men. When they saw that several of the party were wearing German uniforms, they drew their guns and approached more cautiously.

Sergei went forward to talk to the men and, as the armies continued to march by, he explained what had happened. When he was finished, the officer pushed back his cap and whistled once. He saluted Livingston, who returned the greeting, then sent one of his men to fetch a medic. Another was dispatched to brief General K. K. Rokossovsky.

In less than a minute, the general's tank had pulled to the front of the lines. The ruggedly handsome Rokossovsky climbed from the open hatch and, after embracing the two Russians, offered each of the Force Five team members his hand. Lambert also accepted an offered cigarette.

Through Masha, he said to Livingston, "We'd heard of the gas and feared that we would find a dead city. Your courageous actions will long be remembered."

The medic arrived and, after tending to Masha and Colon, treated Livingston's wounds. The lieutenant lay back on the sledge. As far as he was concerned, the bulk of the healing had already been done. These fresh, well-supplied Russian troops would make life miserable for the invaders. He knew the Germans wouldn't roll over and die, but he knew too that they would never take Stalingrad. He looked down the river, squinted into the rising sun, and smiled.

"What's so amusing?" Ogan asked.

"The sun. It's warm. And there's no wind."

Ogan looked around. "An aberration."

"No," Livingston said, drinking in the sight of the soldiers marching past, then shutting his eyes. "A new day."

Chapter Seventeen

The Admiral's Pub was empty this early before lunch. There were ships to attend to, campaigns to plan, fish to catch, and businesses to run. Only soldiers on leave could visit during the late morning, and there were very few of those.

Lambert, Weyers, and Colon were sitting at the bar, nursing beers and wounds.

"Can you believe that mad bastard won't let them surrender?" Weyers asked.

Lambert took a swallow of beer. "Nothing the Führer does surprises me. He was *un idiot* for going into Russia in the first place."

"We weren't?"

"Ours was a noble cause," Lambert replied with a flourish. "Theirs was loathsome."

"But ya gotta admire their guts," Colon said. He was seated at the far end, munching pretzels. "Man fer man, those Krauts ain't pushovers."

"And so many of them are going to die," Lambert said. "How many are left at Stalingrad? Over two hundred thousand?"

"More, I think." Weyers threw his head back, did some rapid calculations. "I make it they'll need about six or seven hundred tons of supplies each day just to survive. Even if Hitler could round up the goods, the Luftwaffe can't spare the planes to carry them in.''

Lambert raised his beer. "To advance planning," he said. "May the Germans continue to leave it all in the Führer's capable hands."

Someone sat heavily in the stool beside Lambert. The Frenchman looked over congenially. His expression clouded.

"I heard you blokes were here. I was afraid we'd miss ye."

In the dark pub, the red beard of the newcomer looked like a mass of sandstone. The eyes were even harder. The fists resting on the faded mahogany were harder still.

Lambert sighed. "Captain Thorpe. How decent of you to welcome us back. I *know* you are a *tres* busy man."

"Very." Two other men moved over from a table in the corner. One carried a blackjack, the other was rubbing a pair of brass knuckles.

Thorpe took a sip from Lambert's beer.

"By all means, help yourself," the Frenchman said. He looked at Colon, who was staring stiffly ahead at the life preservers hanging behind the bar. Weyers was half turned to Lambert, watching from the corner of his eye.

The old bartender came over. "What can I git ye gents?"

"Towels," said the captain. "A lot of them."

"I beg yer pardon?"

"I said *towels*. Y'know—the kind ye use to mop up a mess."

The bartender looked from the captain to Lambert. The Frenchman shook his head. "Don't bother. We're going outside."

"No, we ain't, Rotter."

The five men looked at Colon. Thorpe snickered. '' 'S'matter, mate? Afraid of a fair fight?''

Colon finished his beer. "Bartender, set me up another."

The captain's bushy red brow drooped angrily. "I asked a question, ye Yankee runt. Are ye afraid to fight *fair*?"

"Bartender," Colon said, "you happen to know any American football scores here?"

The burly Scot spun off the stool and walked to the end of the bar, his two men in tow. He leaned on the bar, next to Colon. "Ye were the one who set up that dirty fight, scumbag. I want *you* in particular. Now, are ye gettin' up like a man, or do I have t'*drag* ye from yer seat?"

Colon picked up the fresh stein and took a mouthful of beer. He faced Thorpe—and as he spit the brew into his eyes, brought the stein down hard on Thorpe's hand, which was flat on the bar. The captain howled, and Colon swung his left fist in the man's belly. Thorpe bent at the waist and the glass came down on his head.

As soon as Colon hit the captain's hand, the seaman with the blackjack raised it—only to have Weyers catch his wrist with one hand and break his nose with the other. The sailor stumbled over an anchor and slid to the floor. Lambert beat the third sailor to his feet and, ducking an awkward swing from the man's brass knuckles, locked an arm around his neck and yanked him around, where he met Weyers's massive fist. The seaman seemed to hang on the South African's knuckles for a moment, then fell straight to the floor.

Weyers went over to Colon, who had popped his bandages and was holding his shoulder, wincing.

"You all right?"

"*No!* I really wanted to *kill* the big bastard!"

"I think he means your shoulder," Lambert said as he put several pound notes on the bar.

"Yeah, that's awright. I'll get it fixed."

The bartender walked over. He had been watching

from the door, one foot on the wharf. "Thanks for not bustin' the place up."

"We're not like that," Weyers said. "We're not rowdies."

"Mais non!" Lambert said. "Do we look like the kind of men who would beat up fellow soldiers?"

The bartender studied each of their faces. "Frankly—no." He looked down at the three moaning sailors, then picked up the pound notes Lambert had placed on the counter. He folded them into the Frenchman's hand. "But I've been listening to the things you've been saying—and the next time you *do* fight the Jerries, give them a shot for ol' Dale Rupert. God bless you all."

Lambert was genuinely touched. Weyers leaned over the bar and shook the old man's hand. "Count on me to deliver," the South African said.

"Algeria . . . Russia," the bartender continued. "Any idea where you'll end up next?"

"I wish I did." Lambert smiled. "But they like to surprise us."

Weyers and Lambert headed to the door; Colon paused and, looking down at Captain Thorpe, bent and grabbed a handful of the man's beard. He pulled the round face toward him and lifted the lid of one eye. *"Excremento!* Before we go, there's one thing I want t'say. If we *ever* have the bad luck t'meet again . . . it's *Mr.* Yankee runt to you. Got it, sea biscuit?"

Thanking the bartender again, Lambert went over and pulled Colon onto the dock.

"You know," he said as they walked from the Thames, "compared to Russia, winter in London feels almost—balmy!"

"Speaking of Russia," Weyers said with a frown, "we really shouldn't talk so openly about what we do."

"In the crowded underground, we shouldn't. But in a deserted tavern?"

"Hey, for all we know, that bloke in there might've been a spy."

"Monsieur Rupert? *Impossible!* He was genuinely proud of us. I'll bet he taught some very severe lessons to the Hun in the last war."

"Maybe. But tell me, Rotter. What Englishman in his right mind *ever* parted with a quid?"

"You're being paranoid . . ." Lambert bit off the rest of the sentence and stopped suddenly. *"Merd."*

"What?" Weyers asked.

"How long have we been back?"

"The plane landed one and a half days ago. Why?"

Lambert pointed, and the others stared at Escott's familiar black sedan rushing along Dill Street. The car stopped heavily beside them, and the portly inspector got out.

"I'm glad I caught you," he declared. "You're needed back at the hotel at once. We've got rather a serious problem."

"Where?" Lambert asked.

Escott looked around at the deserted pier. "Norway."

"Norway!" Lambert cried. *"Merci a Dieu.* We'll freeze!"

Weyers and Colon looked at each other and shook their heads. "The man doesn't mind dying, as long as he's warm," the South African said.

Scowling, Escott impatiently motioned the men into the car. And behind them, leaving the shadow of the doorway of The Admiral's Pub, Dale Rupert hurried to the telephone at the back of the bar.

Watch for

Destination: Norway

next in the Force Five *series*
coming soon from Lynx Books!